Chapter 1: Archaic Den

A world of darkness.

That's what the Archaic Densewood felt like after years of growing up in the light and warmth of treetops filled with life. There was a sense of decay and a weight of eyes causing heckles to raise on Oscar and Kiki's backs every few moments. The breeze was unable to penetrate the thickness of the forest leaving the very air to feel claustrophobically close to the skin. The red glow of the moss growing at different angles created ominous shadows in the branches above where Lily walked, her stomach tight and her heart heavy.

"Do you think Mom and Dad are ok?" she whispered out into the darkness, keeping her voice barely audible in case anything was out there.

"They'll be fine," Oscar soothed.

"But, what if they get punished for what I just did? Without Dad putting the ice around my wrists, I would never have been able to use magic." Lily continued, the fear of her parents taking blame for her twisting her stomach painfully.

"I bet Layla and Livius will spread the rumour that you managed to do that yourself and should be feared and despised..." Kiki snarled angrily. The small cat had been in a foul mood ever since they had caught their breath after their escape. Sure, they all knew Lily hadn't exactly been liked by their kind, but the way the whole population turned so easy against a young girl was disgusting.

"It would increase their reasons for keeping you away..." Oscar sighed in agreement.

"I hope so; then they won't do anything to Dad."

As for them, they were left in the darkness, alone with no real knowledge of how to survive and keep going. How did you keep going when everything you knew was gone? Even though she knew the plan was to walk and find Xalina, every step Lily took became more of a struggle, the darkness in front of her seeming to never end. It had only been a few hours since they entered the Densewood, but Lily felt like it was crushing her already. How far had they walked? Were they going in the right direction still?

"One of you should fly above the trees and find out if we're going the right way," she suggested, pulling her mind towards a logical thought rather than a hopeless one.

One foot in front of the other.

If she could keep taking a step, then she could keep moving forward. What had happened was something that couldn't be changed, she was in too deep and the damage had been done. Her body throbbed with the pain of the cuts on her feet, her wrists and the small healing cuts within every bruise on her skin itched in its attempt to heal.

Why hadn't she tried learning any healing magic when she had the chance?? She'd been so fascinated in other daily magic uses, in things that could make her life whimsical rather than anything that could be useful. Lily scolded herself for it now. She'd let happiness make her blind and illogical. She had let herself enjoy friendships and laughter that drew her away from logical learning in the face of a known war. She had let herself be flattered and charmed and her heart stolen by a pretty smile and perfect lies… and she had let that lie guide her in every wrong direction.

Lily had no doubt that Finnigan Byrne had kept her studies on things that wouldn't actually be helpful to her. He wouldn't have wanted to give her an advantage.

Hot tears stung the corners of her eyes at the thought of the brunette male who had betrayed her. He had been so perfect, he had made her feel safe and accepted, he had made her feel confident that she was good enough… but it had all been a lie.

Every single word.

The worst part though, was it wasn't anger that she felt at the thought. It was a sickening acceptance. Because somehow, she must have asked for it. She deserved it for being as pathetic and desperate for acceptance as she was. She hadn't been clever enough to see through him. She hadn't been quick enough to fight back. She hadn't been careful enough to at least keep some part of herself from being owned and thrown aside by him.

The darkness that surrounded her, and the pain that gripped her heart like the fist of a titan were both there because she had failed.

Perhaps it was better to be away from others, at least then she couldn't mess up anything else and bring more hell down on her head.

Kiki landed back down on the ground beside her. "We're heading a little too East, but otherwise we are ok. We haven't got far though; the dark is really slowing us down."

"Maybe we should use some light to at least allow us to walk without tripping up?" Oscar suggested, looking up at Lily with his face slightly aglow from the moss he currently sat upon.

Lily's magic had felt stronger over the last few days, but she had been unwilling to push it by using it as a constant companion. The feeling of it being absent from her body haunted her and she was somehow scared that she could lose it all again if she used too much. But Oscar was right, they weren't going to make any fast movements the way they were going.

Nodding her head gently in the dark, Lily held her right hand out in front of her and pulled the little light around her to one spot which grew until it was a large red orb. As the only light available was red, Lily figured that she'd leave it that way and just brighten it. The orb floated up to head height and moved a couple of feet in front of her, illuminating the woods in blood red hues.

"Well... that's not creepy..." Kiki drawled.

"But we can see where we are walking now," Oscar nudged her in annoyance.

"Uh huh. Sure." Kiki scoffed but hopped over a few unearthed roots that had previously been unseen in the darkness.

"Such a cynic." Oscar rolled his eyes before spreading his wings and flying up to move by Lily's side.

The orb moved at the same speed and distance as it's caster, Lily focused more on the ground than the light itself. But it didn't wane; it didn't even dull in brightness the longer they walked forward. Adjusting the direction, Kiki took the lead and the light allowed them to actually follow each other without Kiki and Oscar having to guide Lily like supporting the blind.

"This is much better!" Oscar chimed happily as he swayed back and forth in the air, his eyes reflecting the orb like a red moon in green pools.

It was certainly easier. And there was something a little smoothing about being able to see at least several feet in any direction.

That soothing feeling quickly vanished at the sound of a snarling to their left.

Two sets of three pink coloured dots in ellipses patterns glowed in the darkness, just out of the reach of Lily's light. Once, then twice, they blinked out of existence for a moment before reappearing with a brighter glow and focus in them.

"What is that...?" Oscar hissed as quietly as possible.

Though that was enough to cause the snarl to grow into a growl and the pink dots to blink once more before the owner of them dove forward into the light, snapping its large fanged jaw closed in the space where Lily had just managed to move her leg from.

The thing was a large creature, its shoulder height reaching Lily's lowest ribs. It had reptilian skin, and its head and back had layers of thick, pale armour that raised up in many areas away from the creature's spine. In the red light, it was difficult to tell its colouring but it appeared to have a different colour to its underside compared to the brown on the top side under the armour.

Its six hooves dug into the ground as it spun to follow Lily's movements. Its breath held the stench of flesh and blood. Not that Lily gave it much thought as she bolted away from the beast, forcing the red orb to fly ahead of her so she could see where her feet were going to connect with the ground.

If she fell, she was dead.

The forest seemed to shake at the roar that echoed when it gave chase. Smaller critters on the ground could be seen bailing out of the way while the sounds from above said that any nearby birds were fleeing. Not that they needed to. Lily was a much bigger and much easier meal. Or she would have been, if the thunderous hooves had gained a little more speed before Lily's mind was able to catch up with her body.

Hooves. It had hooves.

"Get in the trees!" She yelled at the two cats as she pushed off a risen root and leapt up to catch hold of a branch above. For the first time in her life, she found herself glad that she had been motivated to climb and run to make up for her lack of wings. Once up several branches, Lily could settle down on one and sigh as the beast below howled in frustration.

Letting the light vanish from in front of her, she was left with nothing but darkness and the sounds of the beast trying to get up into the tree after her.

Letting out a shuddering breath, Lily pulled her knees up to her chest, barely registering Oscar as he landed on her knees and Kiki on her shoulder.

"We're so going to die..." Lily whispered, each flinch at the noises below causing tears to spill down her cheeks. "There's no way we can do this."

"Of course, we can, we survived that and it can't reach us." Oscar soothed, reaching out with a paw to pat the top of her head.

"And what? We just wait here until something else comes along and kills us instead?!" Lily half shrieked, half sobbed into her knees. She hated this. She felt lost. Scared. Alone. Weak. Her body still stung and ached, the ball of her right foot had been sliced open on something as she ran, the blood soaking into the bark and dripping down onto lower branches.

How was she possibly meant to survive?

"Come on. We've got the truth in that satchel, Xalina will be able to help." Kiki chimed, oddly optimistic. The droll stare she gained from Lily through bloodshot eyes was clearly disbelieving. "And if not, Xalina is a warrior, remember. We'll be safer with her."

Sighing, Lily pressed her face into her knees again, swaying in her seated position as the creature below slammed into the tree in the attempt to knock her out of it. A slim but sturdy branch grew from the trunk of the tree and latched itself around Lily's waist to secure her in place.

"We'll wait that thing out; it'll go for an easier meal eventually." Oscar concluded, hopping up to a higher branch so he could lie down. "We should try to sleep."

Lily scoffed, but made no argument. As if she was ever going to sleep with that thing snarling in the darkness and waiting for her to give in and accept her fate. She didn't want to die, especially not in such a bloody way, but as she sat in the darkness, listening to Kiki's soft snores... Lily could admit to herself that living didn't seem so great right now. After everything, things were supposed to have gotten better, not worse.

The darkness of the forest was oppressive and it was almost impossible to tell night and day apart from under the canopy. Lily spent hours staring up at the dark canopy, watching the little flickers of birds which glowed with bioluminescence strips down their wings and chests, watching what was likely a squirrel moving along the branches silently.

Perhaps she should do the rest of the journey in the trees themselves? It was far more peaceful, and there was a little bit of light stealing through the canopy leaves, giving the world up in the branches a dark green hue. But it was better than the pitch darkness with red spots of light down on the ground.

At what point she dozed off, Lily couldn't say, but when she awoke it was to a stiff back and silence from the tree base. Shifting carefully on the branch, she groaned as her spine and neck made popping sounds in protest. Her left leg had slipped during the time she rested and hung down from the branch. Her right was still in its bent position, her knee having been used as a pillow with her cheek resting on it. Stretching the leg out, Lily grimaced at the feel of the wound on her foot reopening, blood trying to squeeze through the tacky drying scab that had started to form.

Twisting her leg to get a closer look at the cut, Lily pressed a quick kiss to the small cat still curled around her shoulders; a quiet apology for moving while Kiki slept. Freezing the blood over her cut to kill anything dangerous, Lily placed her hand against the branch and focused her magic into growing a long paddle-like leaf that she could bandage her foot. For good measure she bound her left foot as well to help prevent any more cuts. The Archaic Densewood was not as smooth and foot friendly as the mosses that grew on the trees in the Fae Greenwood.

"You should rest more…" Kiki mumbled from Lily's shoulder.

"I ache, and my butt's numb," Lily sighed in return. She was emotionally exhausted, but there were too many jolts of discomfort running through her body for her to settle back down.

"Then we should move some more and rest again in a while." Oscar chimed, stretching out along the branch above them with a large yawn.

"True, can't let her ladyship's bottom suffer too much," Kiki sighed dramatically.

"Plus, that thing has gone." Oscar added. "We should be safe to go back down."

"I was thinking we should stick to the branches. It could be anywhere down there in the dark." Lily commented, finally moving the vine from around her middle and wincing as she got to her feet. "Ki, can you check the direction again?"

With a nod, Kiki spread her dotted wings and jumped up to fly into the canopy.

"Are you alright, Lils?" Oscar asked as Lily straightened herself up and leant her arms on the branch he was sat upon. She turned her silver eyes to the large feline, he didn't really have to ask her that. The cats were bound to her soul, they could feel her fear, her loneliness, and her pain. The guilt of leaving her parents to whatever consequences back home ate at her, and the betrayal of Finnigan Byrne ached like a phantom limb. She couldn't even remotely begin to soothe it, and unlike the abrasions on her skin, she knew that emotional wounds would linger for many years to come.

Lily would have chosen a death by a thousand cuts over the raw agony of trusting someone to the extent she had Finnigan, only to have them rip everything from you and stomp on the still beating heart attempting to survive in her chest.

Despite that, she pushed a small smile onto her lips and lied, "Yeah Ozzy, I'm fine."

Oscar ducked his head a little in acceptance of the answer before nuzzling his head against Lily's cheek. "You know, we're here, no matter where we go or what we do... Kiki and I are never leaving your side."

"I know," Lily sniffled back, turning her head into the soft black fur of her companion. Being in the dark alone without them would have been impossible. "Thank you."

Once Kiki had returned and rectified their direction again, they began to make headway. It was strange to move over branches at a proper height, but it was less daunting than walking through the darkness of the ground. Lily was able to extend branches to cross gaps between trees and thicken them so they didn't break beneath her feet.

They moved without light, and somewhere below they heard the snarl of the beast from before. This time it sounded like there were two of them, and from the yowls of pain, they were fighting. Lily shared a look of fear with Kiki as they silently moved from one tree top to the next until the snarls and growls faded away into silence again.

"I wonder if this place is always so quiet," Kiki whispered. "The Greenwood always has birds and critters making some kind of noise."

"Maybe because of the dark, predators have better hearing so stealth has become vital for survival?" Oscar suggested from somewhere ahead of them. While the tree tops had a little light in them, Lily still couldn't see further than ten feet in front of her and it was all shadowed and blurred together.

"Then, perhaps, we should stay quiet in case everythings' sense of hearing is fantastic and we're being tracked by noise." Lily mumbled, unable to shake the feeling of dread gnawing at the back of mind.

"Good point!"

Rolling her eyes at the smaller cat's response, Lily took her attention off where she was stepping between branches. Her foot twisted as she stepped slightly off to the left of the branch. With a yelp, and a couple of thuds of bone against wood, the white-haired girl clattered down from the treetops and crashed hard into the ground below.

Not onto. Into.

The area of ground she had hit gave way beneath her allowing her to fall another good six to eight foot before finally stopping. Crying out, Lily pushed her torso up to look at her ankle where the pain was radiating most. Her right foot was twisted at a horrible angle and she could see a little bit of her bone trying to break the skin just above her heel.

"Lily! Are you ok?!" She could hear Oscar and Kiki somewhere above her. The pain was blinding and she had no words to give in return. What could she say? No; she was lying in her grave and it was likely that if she even managed to move a beast like before would pick her off like the most pathetic prey to exist? Those words wouldn't form, instead she just hissed and muffled her cry as she tried to move her leg.

"Stay where you are!"

"Oh yeah, like I can do anything else!" Lily snapped in pain before her eyes widened, realising belatedly that that voice had belonged to neither of the cats.

In the very dull light and dirt dust trickling to the floor from the hole she had created, Lily focused on two threatening objects that Lily recognised from history books as battle axes. Immediately her hands rose in front of her with her fingers splayed as though they would be any use as a shield.

Beyond the handles of the axes, Lily could make out the silhouettes of two very small people. They were just over half her own height, and their hair... or maybe hats... were incredibly unruly. Their features remained hidden as the source of light came from another holding a lit torch safe out of reach down the tunnel.

"To your knees! Hands behind your back!" The left person snapped through the dark, their voice a little high pitched as though it hadn't fully matured yet.

Instinctively, Lily attempted to obey, but moving her leg brought her back to reality in blinding agony. Cursing loudly, she shook her head and bit back the tears. "I can't... my foot..." She tried to explain.

"Lily!" Oscar landed beside her while Kiki landed in front, hissing at the strangers with her wings splaying out wide and her fur standing on end. The strangers faltered.

"You're a fairy?"

"Of course, she isn't. She's got no wings."

"Her companions do; and they can talk."

"She's still an intruder."

"And can use magic..."

"Should we cage her?"

Silver eyes darted between the small silhouettes before grabbing hold of Kiki who went to lunge at the closest one. "Don't. I can't do anything with this foot. You'll just get hurt." Looking back to the strangers, Lily held the little kitten close to her. It was very clear she wasn't going to fight them.

"Get a trolley, move her into one of the artefact rooms." The voice furthest away finally said, leaving the other two to complete the instruction. Much to Lily's dismay, they were not careful when forcing her onto the trolley and wheeling her through the dirt tunnels.

Chapter 2: Litihana

The so-called cages turned out to be thick glass containers which artefacts were removed from to make room. Oscar and Kiki were placed in smaller ones while Lily was dumped into the largest one, small slats being pushed open so they could continue to breath. It was a clever place to put her, there were very few of her elements that would help her in such a cage. But mostly, Lily was just disappointed she couldn't get to any plants so she could make a splint for her foot. It was going to be hell to walk on if it started to heal in such an incorrect position.

Groaning from the pain, Lily shifted herself to a sitting position so she could lean against her left leg while getting a closer look at the damage. Moving around had caused the bone to start to break through the skin, the side making her cringe even further in pain.

"Liche!" she cursed under her breath at the tearing feeling under her skin.

"That's only going to get worse. I'll set it for you."

Lily jumped at the voice, her eyes snapping up to meet the brown eyes in a round, kindly face the other side of the glass. There were a few wrinkles, marring the otherwise pale features speckled with dirt and mud, suggesting middle aged years even though the male stood at the same height as the children Lily had known.

"Excuse me?" She squeaked, her cheeks flushed from the pain and effort it was taking not to wallow in it.

The male chortled softly, unlocking the glass container while holding up a box to her line of sight. "I'm the physician, I just want to see your foot."

Not that Lily really had a choice in the matter; either she trusted the stranger or she let her foot set incorrectly and walk in pain forever more. Hissing in pain as she used her hands to move her leg into a more accessible position, Lily found herself sitting with her back against the glass and her silver eyes watching the small hands that reached in to place the metal box down beside her.

"I've never seen a fairy before, but I imagine your bones are like ours, just bigger." The male in front of her was saying as he tentatively began touching and examining the injury.

"And what ARE you?" Kiki called from across the room.

The small male glanced her way, but simply smiled at the rude tone she had chosen to address him in. "Litihana. My name is Kipar Sanrak, I'm the doctor to this section of our lands. We just keep artefacts here, so there's not much for me to tend to."

"Litihana? I've never heard of them?" Lily mumbled, casting her mind back to all the books she had read at Quintegia.

"Well, of course not. We keep ourselves to ourselves and far away from your wars." Kipar commented. Lily couldn't argue with that, that was a safer option.

"The war is a lie." She heard herself saying in a tone that screamed the defeat in her heart.

"Pardon?"

Hands stilled as brown eyes looked up to meet her silver ones. Clearly this was not a statement Kipar had been expecting to hear.

"The war is based on a lie. Neither side actually wants to go to war, they just think they are defending themselves." Lily stated louder, her hands gripping tight around the satchel they had allowed her to keep.

"Your races hate each other..."

"They do. We've painted each other as villains when the real people benefiting from the wars are hidden within both kingdoms." It only took a curious hum for Lily's unrecognised frustration at the situation to show itself. "It's one messed up family that's doing it. They are harvesting magic from corpses to make their bloodline eternal! They've got members in the witch world and the fairy world and they've got us blinded by history and controlled by fear."

The angry tears that pricked at her eyes were foreign. Sadness she knew intimately, but anger... she couldn't remember a time she had felt the boiling heat of the emotion simmering inside her. It was all a lie! Her family, her friends, a whole number of innocent strangers... they were all going to die because of the lies and greed of one family! She could see the lack of care in Finnigan's eyes as he had left her in that room to be drained of her magic. He hadn't even cared after the amount of time he had known her, after the length of time he had spent winning her heart and loyalty.

Lily had no doubt the living members of that family would watch a war kill strangers without so much as a flinch of regret.

"They have got themselves high level positions and they continue to feed the lies so that every century they can use our magic in this insane spell!" Pulling the journal out of the satchel, Lily flipped the pages through to the list of spell ingredients and held it out to the Litihana. Before glancing up, his small hands snapped her bone back into the correct position. A high scream of pain and surprise left the white-haired fairy, dragging tears from her eyes and the sudden adrenaline adding to the pool of anger she was already feeling.

"Liche!" She cursed angrily, leaning her head back and taking in deep breaths through the dizzying pain that throbbed up through her nerves.

"Sorry, figured I should do that while you were distracted." Kipar smiled sheepishly, mopping up the fresh blood that could now seep from the free space in her wound. "Unfortunately, that story won't convince many. Even our history books claim that this was all started because witches and fairies turned against each other. Fairies were losing their wings and witches were losing their homes. It was a world where races turned savage against each other."

"But witches don't use fairy wings for anything..."

"You can have a look at our history records, accounts from those years written by our ancestors if you want. But both races were vicious in their war and it led to the extinction of non-magic humans. It escalated and anyone who got in the way was slaughtered in the midst of it." Kipar sighed softly and shook his head. "Our ancestors ran, it was the only way to survive without possessing any magic to protect us against the rage around us."

"But..."

"Even if you are right and two people did start it; the fact remains that there has been a slaughter every hundred years that people aren't going to forgive anytime soon." Kipar continued. "But you already know that. You wouldn't be in the Densewood if people back home believed you."

The way his eyes met hers steadily made Lily feel like she was being through like one sees through the very glass of the box she sat in.

"They banished me for conspiring with witches..." She admitted gloomily.

"And witches will already see you as the enemy." Kipar stated, turning his focus back to the injury he was treating. "You would be naive to think that one child could change the minds of two races who hate each other."

Was he right? Were fear and history deep enough within the souls of both fairies and witches that they would be too blinded in their hate to even give truth a moment of their time?

Maybe the war was driven by distrust and fear; and the family were just profiting off it. Lily wasn't certain that they would have been the actual cause of the original war; it was a gut feeling and one with very little evidence. All she knew was that they were fuelling the wars to continue. Lily thought back to how Finnigan and Layla had both twisted Lily's situation to fuel the distrust further. Finnigan would have let it out in the witches' world that she had been a spy with ill intent, while Layla had spun her discovery of incantation magic as corruption by witches.

Kipar was probably right; she would be more likely to be arrested or killed than listened to if she went back to either world to try and make someone listen. Rubbing the scabbed wounds around her wrists, Lily let her head fall back against the glass behind her.

"What do I do then?" She asked, not really expecting a reply. The rollercoaster of emotions between anger, fear, sadness, hopelessness, and hope was wearing her down quickly with how suddenly one emotion would transition into another. The overbearing emotion that came with all of them, though, was the daunting feeling of being overshadowed. Kipar was right; she was one person, not even an adult yet, and she was now rejected from both communities involved in the war. Who was ever going to listen to her?

"Well, you won't be able to walk for a few weeks. After that, I'd suggest you leave for the mainland and escape the war altogether."

"Mainland?" Kiki chimed up, mirroring the confusion on Lily's face.

"You really are sheltered, aren't you?" Kipar laughed. "This is just an island - it's a fair distance from the mainland, but this isn't all there is in Ryvalia."

"Ryvalia?"

"It's what those on the mainland call this world."

"So, they aren't at war too?" Oscar called from his glass box, receiving a shake of Kipar's head.

"No," He started. "They aren't exactly integrated together as races but there isn't a war anymore. Hence my suggestion to escape if you aren't welcome anywhere on this island." Tightening up the bandage around Lily's foot, Kipar finally moved away from the glass cage and packed up his tools. "I'll bring you some food."

With that, he left the three with the revelation that this world was so much bigger than they had ever guessed. Their kind knew so little of the world, living in a protected but blind and naive bubble in the treetops, thinking they were in the only safe place from everything else that was monstrous.

"Maybe we should go?" Kiki offered her thoughts first.

"What about everyone else?" Oscar countered. "Mum, dad, Lily's friends?"

"We could go back for them first?"

"And get arrested within moments? That would be suicide."

"Staying here where there is a stupid war, where no one will listen is suicide too!" Kiki snapped. "At least on the mainland, there might be safety."

The bickering reflected well the own argument going on inside Lily's head. The desire to run to the mainland and be away from the pain, the betrayal of Finnigan, the banishment from home, was incredibly tempting. But could she really go knowing that those she did love would be suffering in her wake?

No.

No, she could not. Even if every fibre of her being wanted to run to another place and start over... her pain was not as vital to stop as her parents' potential pain.

"We can't leave," she stated loudly, shuffling to the door of her glass cage which Kipar had left open. Hanging her legs over the edge and sitting more comfortably Lily cast a defeated look over at the cats. "You know we can't. How can we walk away without trying?"

"We have tried. We got banished!" Kiki snarled. "Besides, why would we try so hard for people who have made your life awful?!"

"Because there are also people who made it good." Lily stated with solid conviction. "Even if they now think I'm the enemy, Dia and Tanith are still good people. The teachers, like Wild Witch Agora… they don't deserve to die because of a lie. Even those like River don't deserve to die just because they weren't kind to me."

"Hmph." Kiki flopped to a lying position with a sulk.

"You're a good person, Lil." Oscar commented proudly, raising his rear paw to scratch at his left ear.

"Not really… We just have nothing else to lose," Lily sighed. Banished, battered, betrayed, bruised… It wasn't like there was a guarantee that the mainland would be better. "Everyone else has still got everything to lose to a war."

"It's not your job to save everyone," Kiki reminded gently.

"It is if I make it my job…" Lily mumbled, at least it would mean that she had a purpose to keep moving forward one step at a time.

"Well, we can't do anything until you are healed." Oscar spoke up before Kiki could argue further. "You should try and get some sleep, Lil."

Sleeping on glass was a dream compared to the cave floor she had slept on last, but after a week of sleeping in it, Lily had shifted herself onto the softer ground which had a light dusting of soil at least. Kipar returned every morning and evening to check her wounds and bring her food. The rest of the Litihana sent her suspicious or dirty looks whenever she saw them through the doorway, but not one of them came to talk to her.

When she asked about this Kipar explained that Litihana had sworn to keep their lives in the underground tunnels of the world and leave any of the big folk to whatever destruction they brought upon themselves. They had trouble feeling secure and safe around those who were both bigger and considerably more powerful than themselves.

"Even on the mainland," he had said, "we keep ourselves underground and secret. Those on the surface have a life reliant on magic and could easily destroy us if they chose to. So, we keep ourselves to ourselves and live in peace in the tunnels of the Great Snake."

It turned out that Litihana revered the legend of the Treanguis as a deity. Their legends claimed that the tunnels they now inhabited and expanded were originally burrows of the giant three headed creature. Lily wondered why none of the Litihana had ever seen it if they were living in its burrows, but she politely kept that to herself as Kipar supported her out of the room she had been in and into another where ancient copies of books were kept. They had obviously deemed that she was not a threat, and Lily followed their wishes to use no magic in their home.

Lily found herself oddly fascinated when she read the accounts of the Great War from the view of the Litihana. It was obvious that the writing had been done by one of youthful mind. It was a story of fear and loss, written in the form of a child's diary. The writer described the world as fire and blood, and had been told by their mother to take their younger brother and run for the woods for shelter. From the way the diary read, it wasn't just Fairies and Witches who were in the war; dragons were said to have been vicious in the protection of the mountain area, non-magic humans had attempted to stand their ground but ended up adding to the number of bodies strewn in the path of children who fled for cover. Not one of the parents ever came for them when the war had died down and the children dared to venture out of the tunnels they had lucked upon.

Five of the eldest in the group had ventured back towards their homes to find their parents, only to find ruins of homes and confirmation of their orphanage.

Grieving, alone and scared of the world above ground, the children took to living underground, inventing ways to get around and gather enough food to survive. It was no mystery now why the Litihana were so small, they had been stunted in growth by the tunnels they took shelter in and over time they must have evolved to be smaller to accommodate their environment.

"I wonder how the Draconians saw the war... no story has been the same; apart from the level of death." Oscar mused one evening as he curled up beside Lily's leg to support it while she slept.

"Quintina and Cyrus have so many lives to answer for." Kiki spat.

"Assuming they did actually start it..." Lily countered sleepily.

"Even if they didn't, they've still continued it and killed millions." Kiki growled, still unwilling to budge in her anger at that family. The bruises on Lily's skin from Finnigan had grown darker each day and it had only made the kitten-sized feline sourer.

"Xalina will help." Oscar soothed with a finality that told them both it was time to stop debating who deserved what and get some more rest. Getting Lily healed enough to move again was the larger cat's priority.

It took a couple more weeks until Lily was able to move at least awkwardly. Her ankle couldn't take her weight, but it no longer screamed in agony at any small movement the rest of her leg made. The Litihana still avoided her whenever she moved through the tunnels, though Kipar had become something akin to a friend in the darkness of the underground. He would sit with her and show her how they had designed tools to deal with daily life. He taught her how to start a fire without magic and how some plants from above ground could be harvested for oily sap which would let torches burn for long periods of time. He provided boots which Lily was allowed to use magic to grow to fit her size. He also built a contraption that would be strapped to her calf in order to keep her foot in place and off the ground, while taking all the tension of walking from it. It was made of stone and wood to keep the whole thing rigid, though the part that extended past her foot was slightly springy to withstand impacts and work with the movements of walking rather than against them.

"This is ingenious..." Lily breathed as she examined the contraption around her injury. It held her foot perfectly still which provided a sweet relief of no longer having to fear every small movement.

"Living without magic, we had to get creative." Kipar chortled as he packed away his tools. Creative was certainly a word that Lily would use to describe the Litihana race. She had been told about the community hollows under the centre of the mainland which they traversed with equipment to carry them up and down the levels and to speed up movements through long tunnels with the use of carts. They relied solely on their own to thrive; they didn't train animals, nor did they use magic.

It was an eye opener; to think about how to solve things without an easy answer. Perhaps if she thought outside the box as much as they did, she would be able to find more ways to live easily without wings.

"But you have nothing that could help reduce the losses in war?" Oscar asked the night before Lily was planning on leaving the underground community.

"We have armour that can reduce the impact of magic, but if we gave that to others it would probably just make the wars more violent." Kipar shrugged, though Lily wasn't sure that was the real reason. She suspected that the Litihana wanted to keep that armour a secret so that it couldn't be overcome. They seemed single-minded about keeping their kind safe from the magical races.

"What's it made of?" Kiki ventured, gaining a suspicious look from the male she addressed.

"We call it Hiseki."

Even if he had given the proper name, Lily wouldn't have known how to find and use it. But she placed a hand on Kiki's head when the feline moved to ask more. Despite their need to stay away from the above land, Kipar had helped Lily plenty and she was not about to put a dampener on that just before leaving.

"It could have been useful," Kiki hissed at her later.

"We don't know how to make armour even if we knew what it was." Lily countered with a sigh. "Besides, I don't fancy annoying the people who have given me a way for my ankle to heal without killing me with every movement I make."

"You're too polite for your own good."

"I don't need armour to survive, the idea is to stop the war so it wouldn't be needed anyway."

"It would have helped with the Viparterka…" Kiki countered sourly, shuddering at the beast they had escaped in the darkness. According to Kipar, they were the largest and most vicious predator within the Archaic Densewood.

"Kipar confirmed they can't climb."

"I suppose, though I'm still concerned that this contraption isn't going to make climbing easy for you either." Oscar added as he nuzzled himself closer to the injured ankle to provide extra warmth while it healed.

"I'm sure it will."

"Polite and trusting." Kiki murmured with a roll of her eyes before curling up on Lily's lap to sleep. The words echoed heavily in Lily's ears; perhaps she was too trusting. She had been fooled and played by Finnigan because of it; she had trusted that all the elders wanted the best for the fairy kingdom, she was trusting that Xalina could help her, and she was trusting the Litihana not to have given her the ankle support that would give up in a couple of days.

Was she foolish to trust others? Was it wrong to see the good before seeing the bad? Her life had been filled with people who were not worthy of trust, but there were those who she still believed in with everything she was. Her parents, Dia and Tanith, Xalina… she couldn't deny that she trusted them all still even if she couldn't have most of them in her life anymore. But then, had someone asked her if she trusted Finnigan a couple of months ago, she would have answered that she trusted him with her life... and it had almost cost her that.

The bruises had faded over the weeks, but Lily could still feel the binds she had been in, could feel the restriction around her neck and wrists when she closed her eyes. They haunted her dreams alongside the sparkling of Finnigan's eyes.

She didn't want to experience it ever again; but more so, she didn't want anyone else to experience it. No one should die or suffer just for one family to extend their corrupt lives. So, she awoke from each dream with a mixture of fear and determination curling in her chest. They motivated the next steps she took out of the exit which Kipar waved her through, back into the Archaic Densewood.

"Good luck!" He called before ducking back into the tunnel and caving the entrance in so Lily could not come back.

Adjusting the crutch she was given to support her while her ankle was bound, Lily glanced around the darkness before gripping onto a vine to help her up into the tree line once more.

Chapter 3: Perdiauxilio

Oscar had been right in his prediction, moving with the contraption was difficult, the crutch not much support on the thin branches. But her ankle didn't hurt unless she actually knocked it against something. Movements were slow and careful, attention focused on footing rather than direction.

Not that moving would have been quick if she wasn't injured. The forest seemed to become denser with every step; each tree had to be fought through with magic in order to get to the next branch. Viparterka loitered on the ground's surface in greater numbers and their snarls and growls while fighting over a kill seemed to come from all sides. They quickly deemed the surface level of the forest too dangerous to try and find food in, the cats were chased off prey very quickly before they became prey themselves. The glowing mushrooms, while numerous, caused a violent vomiting reaction from Lily when she tried one.

Water was easy to draw from plants, but despite their thirst being quenched, Lily was soon feeling the effects of starvation. They say that, without other factors, a fairy could survive without food for up to two months, however, after weeks of travelling in what seemed like circles, Lily felt weak and she had begun to lose weight that she couldn't afford to lose. Her body was trying to find the energy to heal and her will was trying to push it to move as well.

Hunger was making them all weak. Every movement, every use of magic, every breath, they were all so much effort.

"Why is this forest so big?" Kiki whimpered one night as Lily collapsed inside the wooden cocoon she had built in the tree tops to keep them safe while they slept. She no longer had the energy to complete it, and so it was more like a hammock expanded from one branch, but it kept them away from the ground-dwelling predators.

"They got the name right though..." Lily chortled sleepily.

"Yeah, Densewood is accurate. I miss The Greenwood though; at least there we could find decent amounts of food." Oscar sighed. "I don't know about you, but even leftovers from the Viparterka kills are starting to look good."

"Even though they are rotting?"

"Yeah, that's how hungry I am."

"I wonder if it could be cooked to a healthy enough level to eat."

"We'll have to try something..." Lily nodded with a small groan. Rotting meat was even less appealing than normal meat which didn't agree with her stomach in large quantities.

"Yeah, I think I'm starting to hallucinate," Kiki batted at a wisp-like orange tuft that had appeared floating above the branch below her.

"I can see them too," Oscar commented as he eyed up the second one that appeared next to it.

"I don't think that's a hallucination," Lily motioned to the two sets of orange glow in the branches above. Within a few seconds, each pair was followed by three orange rings waving back and forth through the air as if they were caught in a breeze.

"What?" Kiki attempted to swat the rings and wisps away as they moved up to her branch and circled around her. The other two were descending on Lily and Oscar, causing both to back away as much as the branch hammock would allow.

Then glowing pawprints appeared on the bark beneath the orange shapes, lingering behind a trail that showed the directions of the movements.

"They're Perdiauxilio..." Lily breathed, remembering the story that Finnigan had told her about them being the finders of lost souls. The moment she named them, slim black felines appeared where there had previously been nothing. The orange wisps were tufts of fur on their long-pointed ears, and the rings were a pattern that ran up each of their tails. The Perdiauxilio were hairless and smooth, they looked like they would have felt like silk to touch, but as Lily reached out to the one closest to her, it shied just out of reach.

"What do they want?" Kiki asked nervously, jumping down onto Lily's shoulder.

"Well, we're lost... maybe they'll show us out of this place." Oscar ventured, his stomach gurgling loudly at the idea of getting somewhere he could eat something substantial.

"Or maybe they'll lead us somewhere we'll be lost forever." Lily countered, recalling Finnigan's theory about the children being taken forever back in the war.

"No, wait. What if the children that were led away by them are the ones who became the ancestors to the

Litihana? These things may have led them to the tunnels where they would be safe?"

"Those tunnels aren't exactly easy to find." Kiki agreed.

The three of them turned to look at the Perdiauxilio who had come to a standstill in front of them.

"We're lost either way… neither of us can get through the canopy to find a direction, at least they'd guide us somewhere." Oscar sighed with a small shrug. "Worth the chance, I reckon?"

"Can't we sleep first?" Kiki whined, surprised the moment the three creatures nodded in unison as though understanding the language.

"Ok. So, sleep, then we get out of here." Lily agreed, settling herself carefully back into the wood hammock without knocking her foot. In turn, the Perdiauxilio jumped up onto a higher branch where they faded from sight, leaving only the orange patterns aglow in the darkness of the foliage.

Considering their position when Lily woke a few hours later, they probably hadn't moved an inch the whole time. They were just waiting for their chosen charge to be ready to move wherever they would lead them.

"They're really… ominous?" Kiki mumbled under her breath as they turned to jump down the tree to lead on the ground.

"Yeah, I think we should follow from above," Oscar added, the glow of the pawprints left behind were easily visible in the undergrowth so long as Lily stuck to the lower branches.

"In case they are actually a lure for prey!" Kiki hissed as though a conspiracy was afoot.

Lily chuckled a little at the dramatic twist Kiki was putting on the situation. Though, given recent events and her luck, they probably would be leading them to something bad. If they did, Lily would just have to do what she'd successfully done twice now... run away. She couldn't exactly see herself as a fighter, but she had gotten away from Finnigan, and then away from the Fairy community when they had chased her. Oh, and the Viparterka. Maybe she'd survive long enough to get to Xalina just by running away from everything dangerous.

"Even if they are, we'll be ok" Lily reached out to ruffle the fur at the base of Kiki's tail with a tired smile on her lips. "We'll just keep going. One foot in front of the other."

They would make it. Somehow, they would make it.

It took a few more days to reach the edge of the Densewood, in which Lily and the cats did end up savouring the number of berries they could find to eat. Oscar and Kiki both managed to catch a couple of small flying creatures as the woods became less dense.

They had lost weight, but the warmth of the sun was as fantastic as ever the moment they bustled out of the woods and into the sparse area between woodland and mountain. It was cooler outside of the Densewood, the breeze licked over Lily's skin and its freshness was enough to make tears prick at her eyes once more.

The damp of the Densewood was obvious in those seconds, the lack of air and the oppressive height of it. Looking at the tundra environment in front of her, it felt like she had been freed from a prison she hadn't known she was in.

For the first time since the truth had come out about Finnigan, Lily felt a sense of freedom that was unusual. She was acting for what she felt was right, and the world was right at her feet. The sparse lands and then the mountains. The clean air of a path that wasn't being shackled in chains by society, expectations, or actual chains.

"*Sokari!*" A voice to the side called out followed by a small chorus of "*Mariatio!*"

The shockwave was aimed above her, shattering branches and leaves from the overhang of trees she stood beneath. The transmutation spell immediately transformed the falling debris into a shower of daggers.

Cursing loudly, Lily flung her arms over to protect the cats in front of her, a slab of wood growing out from the woods behind to cover them and take each dull stab of the sharp weapons.

Her eyes settled on the group of witches that had sent the spells. Six of them were advancing on her from downwind with their wands held in front of them.

Instantly, Lily thrust her hand out in their direction to create a wall of ice to work as a barrier. What she hadn't noticed was a seventh person approaching from another angle. A hooded figure sent a thin metal wire flying at her arm, slicing into her skin and trapping her arm tight against the wood she had used for protection.

A scream ripped from her throat as the wire cut deep into her flesh and blood dripped down her skin. The two cats immediately jumped up to try pulling the wire back from her skin, resulting in small cuts in and around their own mouths.

"You'll rip your forearm off before you'll get free of that." All three froze as a chill of dread fled through Lily at the voice that haunted her mind. Turning to the hooded figure, she could recognise the green of Finnigan Byrne's eyes instantly.

The boy she loved was leading a hunting party to track her down. The clenching of her heart and chest somehow hurt more than the wire which was almost reaching the bone at the side of her forearm.

"If you are here to kill me, why didn't you just do it last time?" She found herself snarling through gritted teeth, the pain within her voicing itself as venomous anger. How could one person toy with her so badly, both with her life and her emotions?

A flicker of hesitation shone in Finnigan's eyes causing Lily to tilt her head as she watched his hooded face.

"You can't, can you?" Or maybe he just won't. Finnigan may believe in his parents' aim but he hasn't become a murderer yet. There was something in his eyes that gave away the innocence of the boy he was. A hesitation that either stemmed from a wish not to actively kill, or perhaps from the fact he had bonded with Lily. Maybe he couldn't face being the hand that ended her life.

Right now, the reason didn't matter.

Using the hesitation to her advantage, Lily froze the blood from her wound and curled the bark of the tree between her and the weapon to pull it loose enough around the arm to rip her arm free, slicing flesh as she went.

"*Peiara!*" Lily flicked out her healthy arm and sent Finnigan flying backwards away from her, though his own hand flew out to bring down the ice that was blocking the rest of the hunting party.

"What?!" Kiki yelped.

"He's half fairy…" Oscar reminded her, raising his heckles in an attempt to ward off the attackers who seemed to ignore just *how* the ice had vanished. His hissing was likely ineffective, however the group seemed to take pause at the sight of Lily casting her arm in ice. A frozen casing to stop the bleeding and numb the pain.

A few beats of silence passed, Lily contemplating how to get away and the witches working out if a front attack was a wise choice.

"*Havatu!*" The slicing spell sent from the redheaded male was met with a wooden wall to take the damage.

"*Agora!*" The fire snake sent from the blonde pixie-cut was doused quickly with water pulled from the surroundings and balled in its path.

Panting, limping and weak, Lily was still able to block the shockwaves, the daggers, and the flames which made up the bulk of the spells being sent her way. None of the witches particularly tried to close any distance but followed as Lily dodged and defended in the direction of the mountains.

She had to get away. She couldn't keep this up. She couldn't use her ice-encased arm and her crutch had been abandoned so the hobbling on her ankle contraption was making her move slow. She either would make a mistake soon, or she would run out of energy to carry on.

Bile rose in her throat as a shockwave knocked her to the side and her ankle jolted.

Fight. Survive. Run. She had to do something. She didn't want to die.

"Lily!" Oscar yelled from up ahead, motioning to the towering mountain and the layer of white that lay thick from about a third of the way up. Dodging another wire aimed for her legs, Lily reached the elevation in the terrain and began to climb.

"She can't move that much at once!" Kiki called from behind as she dive-bombed one witch, snapping the wand in two with her jaw.

No, Lily couldn't.

She was exhausted. It was taking every ounce of willpower to keep her climbing while pulling wood and ice behind her to protect her.

But, it occurred to her, she didn't need to move the ice far. Gravity could do that for her.

"*Bolvia!*" Lily yelled, dragging Oscar and Kiki through the air to her side from where they had been. With them there, she slammed her hand against the ground and cried, "*Sokari!*"

The rumble through the earth beneath her caused the figures behind to stop.

"Are you insane?!" Finnigan yelled over the noise, realising what Lily was trying to do. She wasn't insane, she was desperate. With a look in his direction with eyes full of tired pain, Lily ducked her head to curl around the two cats as a mesh of roots and vines to cocoon them all safely as ice and snow thundered down the side of the mountain in a deadly avalanche.

"They really want me dead..." Lily whimpered as she melted the ice around her arm to look at the damage done. In the darkness of the cocoon, she had to draw light into a small orb above her so she could see, but what she saw was worse than she had thought. In tearing her arm free, she had sliced through the back of her arm and taken chunks of flesh away from bone at either side.

"Tch. We should just leave them to the war!" Kiki spat at the sight of the injury. "We could just go to the mainland and be done with it!"

"It would be the easiest choice..." Lily murmured as she guided thread-thin vines down to her arm and began stitching her skin back together, hissing in pain. She could hear nothing outside of their little safe-space now the snow and ice had covered them, any warmth from the air was gone and replaced with frigid chill. They couldn't stay there for too long, but hopefully they wouldn't be followed now.

"It's not the right thing." Oscar said, nudging Lily's leg to encourage it to straighten a little to be kinder to her injured ankle.

"But we're out here; starving, being hunted, banished, alone! Why should we be the ones who get this deal when everyone else is living a comfy life?!" Kiki growled.

"Because we are no longer ignorant," Oscar sighed. "If we run to the mainland, would we really be ok knowing that the blood spilled in the wars could possibly have been stopped by us? Even if it's just one life that we could have saved?"

Lily sighed as the vines tightened to seal the wounds. She wasn't going to be able to use her arm well for a while, but at least the bleeding had stopped. "He's right Ki... We have to try."

"Tch!"

Oscar shook his head a little at the kitten's response. "You should sling that arm; we'll have to crawl out of this." This being the avalanche on top of them; going straight up would be quicker, but if Finnigan and those witches were close they would spot Lily and the cats against the white of the snow.

Nodding in silent agreement, Lily wrapped vines around her arm and her body to create a stable sling.

"This will be fun, one ankle and one arm out of order..." Lily huffed with a roll of her eyes. She knew Oscar was right, but the idea of running to the mainland and just living was a very tempting idea.

With her magic allowing a tunnel to be created in the frozen covering, Lily was able to leave behind the blood splattered ground and crawl awkwardly on her knees and her one good arm.

Things just had to get better. Lily didn't know how they could get worse.

The tunnel she created took them considerable feet up the side of the mountain before they finally came up for air. The chill had set into the cats who shivered and immediately ran ahead to sit themselves in direct sunlight to warm themselves. Lily could cope with ice a lot better than they could it would seem. Or perhaps she was just distracted by the lightheaded feeling the loss of blood had given her. She could have been cold and she wouldn't have even known it.

Pushing herself to her feet, Lily swayed as her vision seemed to blur before her.

"We've got to keep moving..." She mumbled, mostly to herself as motivation to lift her bad leg and take the first limped step. She would take as many steps as she could. Though how long her body would last, she didn't know.

Blood loss and hunger made moving difficult and slow, every few steps came with a wave of dizziness that brought Lily to a stop with her head in her hand.

"We need to stop," Oscar chimed.

"Where?"

"Anywhere! Create a shelter out of snow or something!" Kiki yelled over the growing wind.

The only problem Lily had was, if she stopped, she wasn't sure she would be able to start again. If sleep took her, she felt that it would take her for good and she wouldn't be able to fight both the tiredness and the injury. Though she was struggling to fight anyway. Her body didn't feel like hers, she felt like she wasn't in control and it was taking all of her will just to keep her legs moving.

She didn't know how long they managed to walk. It could have been minutes or hours. With just one mantra repeating as though to force the movement that sounded out a crunch of snow beneath her.

One step. One more step.

The sensation of her face hitting the soft snow was the only thing she registered as her body stumbled and fell to the white ground. Her legs wouldn't move any more, she couldn't feel her hands, she couldn't hear the cats or feel them by her side.

Dark shapes started to grow in her vision among the falling snow. None of the three blobs would take any focus in her sight, in fact they only got more blurred as they drew closer.

"Xa...Xalina..." Lily couldn't be sure if her lips actually moved to form the word as the shadow of the figures loomed over her. "Please... Xalina." Darkness consumed her sight and the cold of the snow vanished from her skin along with every other conscious sensation.

Chapter 4: The Dregana

The feeling of warmth on her skin soothed her body but pulled her mind back to consciousness. It both made her feel safe but at the same time it took away the numb feeling around her limbs. The sting, the throbbing and the stabbing of different pains caused Lily to groan uncomfortably where she lay on a soft patch of ground.

"Well, you've been through hell."

Lily sat up instantly, raising a hand defensively at the sound of a voice. Her vision blurred and went black at the sudden movement and her stomach churned angrily.

"Whoa! Easy." The voice spoke again, this time accompanied by hands settling on Lily's shoulders to keep her steady. Blinking stupidly in the direction of the voice, Lily could do nothing but wait those moments it took for her vision to come back. When it did, she found herself looking into purple eyes on a cocoa-skinned face with purple scales under the right eye.

"Xalina...?" Lily breathed.

"Hey Lil." Xalina chuckled, taking one hand away from Lily's shoulder and sitting back a little. Glancing around, Lily found the force of warmth. A small yet glorious fire sat in the centre of the cone shaped room they were in. There was a small hole in the ceiling where the smoke from the fire was released, but otherwise the room was sheltered and kept cosy away from the frigid mountain she had been on. Lily spotted Kiki and Oscar snoozing by the fire, her eyes prickling at the relief she felt to find them ok.

Finally, her eyes wandered over to the figures in the doorway, standing with their back to her and Xalina as though acting like guards.

"It's ok. I told them you're a friend but they wanted to speak to you before taking the guards away." Xalina commented, drawing Lily's attention back to her. It was the first time Lily had seen the Draconian in a proper lighting this close. Her hair was a beautiful violet colour that shimmered in the light of a dancing fire; it had a gentle wave to it that Lily's straight hair could never have and it settled just below her shoulders.

"Them?" Lily questioned, taking a moment to catch up with the words that were spoken.

"My tribe." Xalina chortled. "They found you on the mountain side and said you'd asked for me... so I explained what you were trying to do at the school and that you weren't dangerous. So, they've been healing you." She motioned down, causing Lily to inspect the state her arm was now in. It was properly bandaged and the sting was no longer there, as though some cooling ointment had been used to soothe the pain.

"They said the stitching was good... but made of plant material?" Xalina continued with a raised eyebrow.

"I didn't have much else to use..." Lily mumbled, though she didn't expect a bright laugh to come from the entrance.

"I always knew you were a badass!"

Lily's head snapped around, her eyes widening in shock as she focused on the owner of the voice, the cropped black hair, the dark blue eyes...

"Tanith?!" Lily's face spread into a surprised smile at the face she hadn't expected to see.

"In the flesh!" Tanith replied, striding over to take a seat beside Xalina, unabashedly greeting her with a kiss to her cheek and gaining a kiss to her nose in return.

"You're Xalina's partner?" Lily voiced out what was an obvious question, and she received a droll, sarcastic raised eyebrow for it.

"No. You don't say!" Tanith laughed.

"So, did you...?"

"Know you were a fairy the whole time? Yeah, we have no secrets." Tanith chortled, though Xalina did glance at Lily with a slightly sheepish expression. "I was doing some digging back at home to see if I could help and then the alarm went through the kingdom that you had attacked the main city. Which obviously was insane! But everyone seemed to believe it..."

"Everyone?"

"Everyone."

The look between the two girls was all that was needed to know that by 'everyone' they both meant 'Dia'. Lily sighed. Dia believed Lily had used her, and had been the villain of a story she wasn't aware was playing out. Which meant she believed that Finnigan was a victim and possibly a hero for being willing to turn against his villainous 'ex-girlfriend'.

Tanith reached out and ruffled the white locks on Lily's head before offering her a smile. "We know you ain't a bad one though, right?"

Lily chuckled and nodded. She didn't want to be hated by everyone, but she did know in herself that she wasn't the villain here.

"What happened?" Xalina asked gently, motioning to the injuries. Lily the recounted her side of the story; explaining that the small dots over her body were from the peyadu when Finnigan had turned on her, that the scarring on her wrists was from when she was arrested by her own kind, the ankle was an accident and the newest ones on the sides and back of her arm were from Finnigan once more.

"He's hunting you?!" Tanith growled out at the end. "So, he tricks everyone, uses you, betrays you, breaks your heart and now he's leading teams to kill you? I'll throttle him myself!" She had gotten to her feet and started pacing, and her fists were now balled tight by her sides as though there was nothing more she wanted than to punch someone... Well, not someone, Finnigan. "I don't understand. I saw how he looked at you! That was love on his face! How can someone lie that well?! Liche!!"

Both cats jolted awake at the insult that was yelled by Tanith, immediately jumping up and hovering in the air with their hackles raised.

"Sorry, don't mind me," Tanith commented, continuing her pacing.

"Lily! You're awake!" Kiki said excitedly, flying over to the fairy and landing in her lap purring.

"You had us seriously worried there," Oscar added, nuzzling his head against Lily's when he reached her. Lily turned her head to let his fur cover her face as she nuzzled him back with a mumbled apology, her good arm moving to stroke over Kiki's fur. They were so warm and she could feel their little heartbeats strong under their skin.

"I'm glad you guys are ok." She whispered softly, relief making her immediately tired once more.

They were safe. Finally.

As though her body knew that fact, her stomach soon drowned out Tanith's grumbling with a loud gurgling demand that caused both Xalina and Tanith to snort with laughter.

"I'll get you some food." Xalina chortled, pushing herself to her feet and exiting the room.

Lily turned her attention to Tanith and tilted her head. "How come you didn't tell me?"

"Huh? About Xal?" Tanith finally settled herself back down on the soft floor which looked like the coat of a wild beast. "Yeah, sorry about that. I figured it would be something difficult to talk about without Dia getting suspicious why we couldn't tell her something. Besides," she continued, "I guess I got into the habit of never speaking about Xalina in case I got her in trouble. Oh, thanks for springing her from the Lockup by the way."

The smile Lily received was heartbreakingly soft. It was an expression that somehow seemed surprising on Tanith's features with all her confidence and wild aura. The only thing anyone should be able to do in the face of that kind of love is smile, and that's exactly what Lily did. She couldn't help it; one of the people she would class as a best friend looked so gentle and happy to the core of her soul when she looked at the Draconian walking back into the room.

Xalina handed over a bowl of hot broth that smelled rich and spiced, it was all Lily could do not to drink it immediately and scold her throat.

It was blissful. The heat of the broth warmed her to the core, the spices brought pink to her pale cheeks, the scent awakened her mind and memory to the warmth of meat dishes in the winter months at Quintegia, the laughter that had surrounded her.

"This is amazing..." She sighed out after half of the bowl was gone and her stomach was gurgling with the effort and eagerness to digest something other than its own lining.

"I am surprised that a Fairy could stomach our spices." A calm voice came from the entrance to the room and all eyes turned to face the owner. Their hair was as white as Lily's but their scaled wings were dotted in pale blue patches much like areas over their weathered skin.

"Ah." Xalina got to her feet to give some kind of greeting which involved curling her left hand into a fist, bringing it to rest against her lips and bowing her head. Tanith did the same motion from where she sat. Once the elder had repeated the action in response, Xalina continued. "This is our Dregana, she is the head of the tribe."

Lily went to stand to pay her respects, however the pain of her ankle hadn't faded completely and she wobbled and ended up on her knees.

"Oh, do not strain yourself. You've been in quite a battle," the Dregana spoke, her voice aged with wisdom and hard decisions.

"I want you to tell me your story." She added as Xalina helped her to sit on the ground in front of Lily, her fingers interlinking with each other in her lap. "We thought it was unwise for Xalina to be meddling in the affairs of others, and now you are here on our doorstep. I would know your story to determine whether Xalina is right in her judgment to help you."

"And, if you don't think she's right?" Oscar chimed.

"We'll burn that bridge if we get to it." The warning in her deep blue eyes was unmissable; Lily was not going to receive any help if this woman didn't deem her cause worthy enough.

Gulping back the dread that threatened to seal her throat, Lily settled herself back into a more comfortable sitting position.

Recounting her story, Lily couldn't help but recall the way Kipar had responded in doubt, anxiety set in that she was going to be met with the same response now.

"It was all a lie based on greed, people don't need to keep dying." Lily finished, her mind tired from recounting the tale, her evidence from her back laid out on the floor. The Dregana was scanning through the journal with the spell requirements and Tanith was leaning over the family tree rolled out on the floor.

"There is much hate between the races…" The Dregana started.

"Yes," Lily interrupted, surprising the others there by the look on their faces. "But someone has to break that hatred; someone has to offer friendship… or it will just continue." Lily glanced at Tanith and Xalina. "Right here in this room we have proof that it doesn't just have to be hatred between races! You two love each other and

I, a fairy, love you both and want to fight *for* you, not against you."

Why couldn't the world see that? Lily sighed. This whole thing had blinded so many, yet no one wanted to fight apart from those who benefited from it.

"It's not that simple." The Dregana said, causing Lily to deflate and slouch herself in her seated position. Why wasn't it that simple? Why were people unwilling to make it that simple? "I don't think your aim is wise, however, you are welcome to take shelter here. Rest, recover, and learn."

"Learn?" Lily repeated.

"You can join our training activities." Xalina clarified as she assisted The Dregana to her feet and once more held her fist to her lips and bowed her head in respect as the elderly female left. "It'll help build up your muscle and physical fighting skills in case you need them."

"I don't want to fight."

"Lil, you're standing in front of a tidal wave that's been going on for years… if you want to keep convincing people of what you've found, you are going to be met with people who don't agree or even those who want to silence you." Xalina sighed. "You won't be able to take this path without a fight."

"You know that already though…" Tanith added, motioning to the bandage around Lily's arm. "If you go back down the mountains, Finnigan is probably going to be waiting."

Lily glanced down at the wound and then across to Oscar who looked back at her with something akin to empathy. Neither of them wanted to fight, neither of them wanted to be in pain or cause pain. Was there no way to do this without that?

"Finish your food, and get some more rest." Xalina spoke softly, reaching out to pat the white fairy on her shoulder in a gesture that was both full of support and sympathy.

"They might be right, you know." Oscar breathed as Xalina and Tanith left them alone to settle back down.

"I know. I just wish they weren't."

"Well, so what if they are?" Kiki chimed with a small growl. "Personally, I think Finnigan and his family deserve a good beating for what they've done."

Lily chortled as the socked-feline batted at an imaginary enemy in front of her as though that would help her point.

"I'm sure you'll teach them a lesson if you get the chance." Lily ruffled Kiki's ears and found her hand pounced on by the feline who was still in the mood for a fight. A play-fight between Kiki and Lily's hand wasn't uncommon and always ended in Kiki pinning Lily's hand to the ground and sitting on it in triumph, never mind the fact that Lily could have still lifted her. Instead, Lily would flail her fingers and exclaim, "Ah, you killed it! You win!" and lay herself down beside the victorious cat so she didn't pull her hand back to herself.

It was a silly exchange, but it lightened Lily's heart considerably. Even if everything else was changing or getting darker, at least Kiki and Oscar were the same as ever.

With Kiki snuggled up over the defeated hand, and Oscar curling up against Lily's stomach, the fairy found sleep.

Chapter 5: Xeomont Peaks

Sleep made up the majority of time usage over the next few weeks. Safe, warm, and fed, her body was allowed to recover properly for the first time in weeks… or was it months since she's found out the truth about Finnigan? Days had merged together in the Archaic Densewood; the only certainty she had, was it couldn't have been any more than a couple of months as her body hadn't lost all of its mass through starvation. The food the tribe provided was rich in nutrients and her body began to fill out again relatively quickly, though she had to eat a small amount more often as her stomach couldn't handle large meals.

Once her leg was fully recovered and she no longer needed the contraption to keep her steady, Lily could venture outside on the ice and snow of the Xeomont Peaks.

Xalina's tribe lived on the east facing side of the mountain and commonly hunted in the early morning when other critters were waking up. Vegetation was fetched by groups who headed down the mountain, these were usually made up of the strongest warriors of the tribe as it was dangerous to go near Witch territory.

The air was beautifully clear up in the peaks even if it constantly held a chill.

The tribe set Lily up with thick clothing made of fur and animal skin which was incredibly good at insulating her skin. She had explained she wouldn't need something so thick, just enough that her body didn't succumb to the ice it was used to… but they had insisted, and the fur lined boots they had provided made it feel like she was walking on fluffy clouds, so she stopped protesting.

They were only being welcoming, which wasn't something she was used to

"Do you want to join our training tomorrow, Lil?" Xalina asked while they sat around a fire over which was a large pot cooking the night's meal for the tribe.

"Oh, you'll have great fun!" A young man chimed up. His name was Xavion, a friendly teen who had been interested in asking Lily about what it was like in the Fae Woodland and Archaic Densewood. Apparently, he was banned from going too far from the tribe because his curiosity of the wider world often got the better of him and he ended up in dangerous situations. Xavion's colouring was red when it came to his scales, the edges of his wings and his hair. Not an auburn like Dia's had been, this was darker and almost intimidating. Or it would have been if the male knew how to give a death glare.

Lily had noticed that the Draconians, as a rule, had blues, reds or purples in their colourings, and the majority had darker hued skin than fairies. Though that made sense as they spent a lot of time outside in the direct rays of the sun above. It was beautiful though, and more than once Lily had found herself wishing she had something more than white and silver on her body. Especially the purple, she liked the purple hues.

"I can try," She agreed, though was really unsure on how well she would keep up with them.

"You're not allowed to use magic to help," Tanith warned.

"I don't mind. I wasn't allowed to use magic with the Litihana at all and I survived." Lily chortled. "It's quite nice learning how to do things without magic though, it's like looking at the world in a new light."

"Deep..." Xalina teased, petting the head of Tanith's snake companion which was settled around the draconian's shoulders.

"It's pretty cool though," Xavion chimed as he handed out the bowls of food to the three girls and sat himself down on the snow in front of them.

"What is?" Tanith raised an eyebrow, glancing up from where she was offering Kiki some of the meat from her bowl; the little feline curled on her lap and gratefully munching on whatever she was offered.

"Well, think about it," Xavion shrugged. "Lily's probably the only one who's experienced all four cultures now. Like, not just knowing about them, but properly experiencing them."

"It's a shame no one seems willing to believe you though," Tanith added in a barely audible whisper. The Dregana had come back after deliberation saying that they couldn't risk standing against the other races on the word of one girl. Once again, the evidence Lily carried had been dismissed.

"Can you imagine living in a world where we could just go wherever we wanted?" Xavion sighed wistfully.

"Could go to the mainland and do that there," Oscar pointed out from Lily's lap.

"We could all go and escape the war completely," Xalina suggested.

"Somehow, if we can't convince them to believe about the races they know exist, I can't see us being able to convince them all to trek to a land that may or may not exist." Xavion laughed with a shake of his head. "Besides, it's not like the Litihana gave Lily directions."

"Yeah, it could be a lie and it's just the Densewood going on and on for years."

"And we almost died there within a month!" Kiki spluttered around a mouthful of food.

Would Kipar really have made up the idea of the world being bigger than this war-torn area? Lily couldn't see why he would have done it, there was nothing to gain from telling her about it. Though, she supposed it was a way to make her think going back to the Litihana wasn't a good idea as they supposedly were not anywhere close in the tunnels and she'd get lost trying to find her way. Had she just been naive again, believing Kipar for his word?

Was she being naive, believing Xalina and Tanith that she was safe here in the tribe and she wasn't about to be sold out? She didn't think they would lie to her… but then, she also hadn't dreamed in a million years that Finnigan would have been lying to her the whole time either.

She had to make the decision whether to trust or not to trust, and there was a voice in her mind that told her trusting people was unwise. Still, she wanted friendship, she wanted to trust those around her and know she wasn't alone.

So, Lily made the conscious decision to put her trust in her friends and the draconians. Joining their training was a good idea to build her strength back up, and it turned out to be a much more intense activity than Lily could have ever imagined.

Draconians were melee fighters who used pole arms. Lily had never even considered having to fight without her magic before, and she did wonder what good it would have done in the face of magic, but the hikes up and down the side of the Xeomont Peaks every morning increased her leg strength and her stamina. Being taught hand to hand fighting and how to disarm an enemy or subdue them without having to actually strike them was fascinating. Her body didn't get bigger, but the knowledge and the skill came with a feeling of security within herself.

"Does this actually work if you are against witches?" Lily asked Xavion one afternoon as he tried to guide her in how to hold a pole arm properly. Her arm was mostly healed and the lightweight weapon was good to train with. The length of it allowed her to use it as a walking aid if her ankle twinged at any point as well.

"I… don't actually know." Xavion replied awkwardly. "We have a resilience to magic, but we don't really see witches often to know?"

"So why train so much?" Kiki huffed.

Xavion blinked down at her with his red eyes and seemed to take a few moments to think about the question. "Because we always have? Makes us feel safer?"

"I think living up here in icy conditions is more likely to keep you safe," Oscar chuckled, swiping snow up at Kiki's face. With a small growl, the smaller feline turned and pounced on the larger.

"That's true; I can't see them venturing up here. I can control ice and I nearly didn't make it because starving made the cold set in. Witches wouldn't even have the help of being resistant to cold." Lily mused. That was the reason she suspected that Finnigan and the others hadn't continued up the mountain after her. Unless they thought that avalanche had killed her? If they did, wouldn't it be easy just to stay up the mountain and never be seen by the witches again?

The answer, of course, was that would be the easy path to take. But Lily knew she couldn't just hide up here. The information she carried in the satchel safely under her fur sheets in the medic tepee couldn't just go forgotten. Not only would the impending war happen, but they would continue to do so every century. That was too much blood to have on her hands just for the sake of her own comfort.

"You ok there?" Xavion asked, bopping her lightly on the top of her head to bring her attention back to reality.

"Yeah. I just... I can't stay here forever." She admitted lamely.

"Why?" Xavion asked with his head tilting slightly. "You're welcome, and it's safe from the war."

"The war shouldn't happen."

"How can you stop it?"

"I don't know!" Lily snapped. That was the big issue. She didn't know how to stop it. She had thought that Xalina might be able to help, but the Dregana had been adamant that the risk was too high even if Lily was right. So, was it really just her? Sure, it wasn't like she had much else to lose... but could she really make a difference on her own?

Sighing, she handed the pole arm back to Xavion and walked away towards the edge of the ledge they were training on. Sitting down to dangle her legs over the side, Lily found herself looking at the vast land beyond. She could see the trees of the Densewood across to the right and she could see a valley at the base of the mountain through the clear air. Everything was so small from this height, but that didn't make her feel any better.

Folding his wings behind him, Xavion came to sit beside her, leaning forward a little so he could look at her face.

"If no one will listen, why is it your responsibility? You've told your kind, the Litihana, and now mine... surely, you've done your part."

"Have I?"

"Haven't you? Who else is there to go to?" The heartbreak in Lily's eyes at Xavion's words was enough to make the male recoil a little and guilt mar his features.

"So, what? I accept that there's nothing I can do to stop people dying in less than three years?!" That couldn't be it! She wouldn't allow that to be it.

"No. You accept that you might be able to save individuals, rather than everyone." Xavion sighed. "You could still save your family; keep convincing our Dregana to take our people to another land away from the war; you could go into the witches' territory and save your friend."

"And let everyone else suffer?"

"One person can't save the world. You'll die trying." Xavion shook his head at the seething look that was deepening on Lily's face. How could he?! How could he so easily condemn so many faceless strangers?

"Then I'll die." Lily said with anger she had never known within herself as she jumped to her feet and stormed off through the training ground.

Her feet took her away from the tribe and further up the side of the mountain. Angry muttering sounded from her lips into the silent cold. What was it with people?! How could they not see what was right? How could they be so blinded by fear that they would allow those they don't know to die?! Her own kind had so quickly believed she was a traitor over the idea that she might have found something to stop a war, Dia had believed Finnigan about Lily using them for information to find their weaknesses, the Litihana, who had magic repelling armour, refused to help save lives, and now the draconians... people who were blessed by dragons themselves... would do nothing but hide in the mountains as blood and death stained the land below.

Fear was a big factor, but the other seemed to be a lack of willingness to believe in anything that wasn't what people had been taught was true.

"How am I supposed to untangle a web this big?" She grumbled, settling herself on a ledge from which she could climb no higher. "There's got to be someone who will help..."

But who? Maybe if she could get back and speak to her parents? Or perhaps Jared... though Jared was Layla Linwood's son so there was a high chance that he was involved and couldn't be trusted. She could go and find Dia and see if she could convince her of the truth.

In reality, she knew she needed adults on her side. But what adult other than her parents had ever been on her side?

"Pfft, they'd all sooner lock me away in a metal crate," she said bitterly to herself.

A flake of snow landed on her nose as the clouds began to build, covering the blue of the sky in a deep, cold grey. Fitting; that was how her heart was beginning to feel with her hopeless train of thought. Blank calmness filled her mind as her eyes followed the soft flakes falling to the snow already coating her boots.

Maybe they were all right… if she left, she could be free. Truly free. She could live for herself and she could make all of her decisions for her own life. She could travel, meet people, discover places, and never have to worry about not fitting in again. Perhaps she could find the other land Kipar had spoken of, perhaps there were even more than just that one. Maybe she could find a place where she wasn't the outcast for not being normal.

It was tempting.

No, it was more than tempting. A large part of lily wanted that more than anything; to belong somewhere. She didn't belong anywhere she had been so far, so maybe there would be a place beyond the horizon where she could just be… well, her. Up here, alone on a mountain top with the horizon right in front of her, she found that she wanted to see what was past it. She wanted to run away from the pain of rejection, of fighting, of lies. She wanted to run to somewhere she could speak her mind without worry of further banishment. The sound of the wind blowing across her face was like a siren call, filling her with a longing that she knew well but was always too scared to do anything about.

Did she follow it this time?

Could she just... leave?

"Lily!"

"Lil! Where are you?!"

"For wings sake! Where is she?!"

The voices of Kiki and Oscar grew louder.

"I'm up here!" Lily called back, the hair on the back of her neck raising fearfully at the tones their voices had taken on.

Soon enough, she could see the black of their bodies against the white background, flying up to her through the increasing snowfall. "Are you ok?!" Oscar yelled before they even reached her.

"Of course, why wouldn't I be?"

"Oh, good. They haven't come up this far." Kiki sighed.

"Who didn't?"

"Witches. They're attacking the tribe looking for you!"

Dread. Horror. Nausea.

"We've got to go!" Kiki stated as Oscar shoved the satchel with Lily's stuff into her arms.

"What? No. We've got to help!" Lily argued.

"They are warriors! You are not!" Kiki barked, pulling at the fur of Lily's coat's collar. "Plus, there's no sign of you there; so, they can claim they know nothing of you. If you go down there, they'll all be killed for assisting you."

"But!"

"Ki's right! We've got to hide!" Oscar snapped, pulling on Lily's sleeve.

With a glance down the mountain where she could see smoke beginning to rise from the tribe's direction, Lily let out an anguished groan before turning and following the cats further around the mountain. They were right, she would be more danger than she would be a help.

"How can anyone be so useless..." Lily grumbled once they pulled themselves through a slim gap between rocks which took them into a frozen cave.

The silence of the cave seemed louder than anything she had ever known as derogatory thoughts spun through her mind. They weren't new, but somehow, they were heavier on her heart now more than they ever had been in her childhood. Perhaps it was because it was her own voice she could hear as opposed to people who didn't really know her.

"Lil..."

"Don't 'Lil' me! I'm the reason the witches came this far and now I'm running away and hiding? How is that not useless?? Or perhaps pathetic would be a better word." Lily paced the length of the cave and back, the ice cracking under her feet and creating jagged, angry lines across the floor and up the walls. She shouldn't be running. The Draconians had been so good to her, had helped heal her, had provided for her... and this was her thanks?!

With an angry yell, the ice lining the walls and ceiling shattered and fell to the ground with an ominous tinkling noise that echoed in the darkness.

"Nope. I can't do this. I'm going back." She stated finally.

"Are you crazy?!" Kiki yelped, flying up to hover in front of Lily's face and stop her moving back towards the entrance.

"I have to do something."

"They'll kill you!"

"So, what?!" Lily snapped, shocking herself with how little she cared about that possibility. With a sigh she shook her head. "You guys really want to live if it's just running away and leaving behind friends and family to suffer?"

Both cats stayed silent.

"We don't want you to suffer..." Oscar offered.

"I'm already suffering."

And wasn't that the truest thing she had said in the last few months. The smile she put on telling Xalina and Tanith she was fine while her heart felt like it was vacant from her chest. The bravado she used to train when her body still had phantom pains shooting through it from her injured arm, and the burns around her wrists that had scarred now. The hours she had spent pretending to sleep while in fact too afraid to in case she had another dream of her neck being held in place while she couldn't fight back.

Hanging her head, letting strands of her hair fall out of where they were tucked into her hood.

"I'm a freak and I'm unwanted by my own kind. The guy I thought loved me has tried to kill me twice. I'm pathetic and just keep running away. I'm even contemplating just leaving because I'm so scared… and I hate myself for it." Because how weak did she have to be for all of this to be pushing her to this point? "I don't want another reason to hate myself."

It was that and the heavy look in her icy eyes that had Kiki deflate with a sigh and nod her head. "Alright. Let's do it."

"We're with you." Oscar chimed from where he had walked over to her and nudged her shin.

"I know…" If they weren't, she wouldn't have survived the bullying as a child, let alone this. "I love you both."

Crunching over the broken ice, Lily shuffled her slight body through the gap before pulling all the ice shards out with her. They seemed to shine even under the dull sky and they held their own against the wind and snow that was increasing by the second. Pulling them in front of her, the shards closed in on one another to form a translucent shield for Lily to keep in front of her and the cats.

This terrain was truly where her creativity from her childhood could shine. Her old method of creating an ice slide to speed her descents on branches, right now, became the snow winding around her feet and shifting her quickly through the flakes of frozen water. So long as there was snow in her path, she could move quickly. It wasn't graceful, but it would get her to the camp quicker.

While Lily, on her own, was hardly a formidable sight; the sight of the thrown-up snow from her movements becoming a small avalanche in her wake was enough to cause fright when she jumped down a ledge to be able to see the camp and those remaining in it.

Instantly, Lily could see that the witches had demolished the camp looking for her. The tepees had been torn down, the weapons and tools were tossed in a pile that burned angrily. There weren't many in the Draconian tribe anyway, possibly sixty at most, and Lily could see a few laying completely still in the snow while the last of the witches dragged a couple of them away in shackles.

"Stop!" Without thought, Lily spread her arms and swung them to a clap in front of her. This movement sped up the avalanche behind her, the snow splitting to avoid her, and send it straight for the camp. It covered the fire, quashing it immediately, and it split around the Draconians so the witches were caught up in its current and taken straight down the mountain.

"That was…"

"Insane…"

She heard the cats murmur at the display but the white-haired fairy paid no attention. She didn't know she could do something that big with her magic, but she also didn't care right now.

Running over to the Draconians who stood stricken, she realised the male was Xavion.

"What was that?!" He half yelled.

"Snow?" Lily answered stupidly, transforming his expression from one of shocked awe to sarcasm.

"Really? I thought it was puppies." He rolled his red eyes with a shake of his head.

"Oh, shut up…" Lily grumbled, lifting a handful of snow and placing it against the lock of both shackles. Concentrating on forming the right shapes and solidifying the ice so it wouldn't break, the locks clicked and the shackles fell from their wrists.

"Mom! No!" The young female darted away from them over to one of the bodies in the snow, tears bursting from her the moment she realised there was no life in her mother.

Lily couldn't look away.

Everything she had thought she was suffering… it was nothing in the face of what she was witnessing. The young draconian was probably younger than her, and here she was, crying over her mother's body while the rest of the tribe were dead or gone.

"I shouldn't have come here." Lily whispered.

"This wasn't your fault," Xavion started.

"They would never have come if I wasn't here. That girl's mother would still be alive!" Lily snarled at the redhead before walking over to the pile in the centre of the camp. "I'll get them back." Leaning down, she pulled a charred polearm from the pile and shook it free of snow. The two cats walked over to her with confusion written on their faces, though to those, Lily gave a slight smile.

"Figured a new 'fancy stick' might be useful." If she could funnel magic through a stick that was wand shaped, there seemed no reason why she couldn't do it through a charred and blackened polearm that came with extra pointy bits. The wood was broken at the end making the point jagged while the metal blade that curved like a scythe remained solid.

"I think that's called a 'scary stick'," Oscar chuckled.

"We're going back into the witches' land... scary might help."

"How exactly do you plan on freeing them all?" Xavion chimed from where he had gone to comfort the grieving girl.

Lily paused. She hadn't thought about that, she had no idea how she was going to face them - or even where they would have gone.

"I don't know. But I freed Xalina, I'll find a way to do it again." Her silver eyes glanced from one cat to the other, receiving a supportive nod from them both. After her admission in the cave, they both knew that arguing to leave it be was going to be fruitless.

Chapter 6: Combat Magic

Where the snow of the mountain melted into the grass of the adjoining lands, it was clear to see the direction the draconians had been taken. The mass of footprints in the damp mud, trapping strands of grass in their wake, couldn't be missed. Draconian footsteps indented the ground deeper than witches, their tall muscular build making them heavier; though there didn't seem to be much sign of struggling.

"Why...?" Lily started, glancing up at Kiki who shrugged while having the same thought process. Why wasn't there more of a fight from the Draconians? With all the training she had seen them do... how could there be such little resistance now they were away from the tribe camp?

"Surely they wouldn't just give up... what would be the point of all their training?"

Over the next few hours, following the crushed grass after the mud had dried up, Lily, Kiki, and Oscar concluded that they must have been threatened into not fighting back. Perhaps the children had been used to stop the adults from resisting.

Their voices halted immediately as a small village came into view ahead of them. It wasn't the settlement that caused their hesitation, but the amount of temporary shelter that had been set up and how many witches dressed in guard uniform were pacing back and forth. Increasing the height of the grass a little more, Lily darted to the side of the crushed walkway and crouched herself in the strands to hide herself from view.

"What do we do now?" Kiki hissed.

"Are they keeping the Draconians here?" Oscar added.

"I don't know," Lily pondered, her eyes trying to focus on the village through the dense grass. With concentration she was able to move the strands just slightly to create a gap small enough for her left eye to see clearly through.

"What if one of us snuck in?" Oscar suggested.

"They are hunting us, if I go in, even in disguise they'll likely be testing everyone somehow. They know I can change my colouring."

"But would they suspect you could change ours? Think about it, you read those books on metamorphosis, if you can change me into a different animal, I would be able to move around freely."

"I've never even tried to do those spells!" Lily squeaked.

"Do you remember them?"

"Yes but…"

"Then try it. It's our best chance."

Lily glanced at Kiki though was met with a look of utter amusement. "Oh, please turn him into something hilarious."

"I was going to suggest a raven or crow as they are common." Oscar replied stiffly.

"I don't remember the word for raven…" Lily shrugged. "I can remember the word for rat, mouse or chicken."

"Oh! Do chicken!" Kiki laughed, slapping her paws over her mouth to try and keep the sound muffled.

"Rat would be better, there's loads of them as well, both wild and companion." Lily chortled at the swat Oscar gave Kiki over the back of her head.

"Not ideal... but it'll do." Oscar sighed, settling onto his haunches showing he was far readier for this attempt than Lily was. Metamorphosis was something she had only read about and it was completely different to transmutation. Metamorphosis involved living creatures, if it went wrong it was going to be far worse than ending up with a book that still had chair legs out the bottom of it. While the idea of Oscar having tiny little rat legs was a hilarious mental image, it would be a horrific reality for Lily to try to put right.

"It's all going to be fine. You've mastered every spell you've ever tried." Oscar said, pulling Lily from her thoughts. "And if you just give me a few rat features, at least Kiki will be in a good mood for a long time." He offered her a soft smile while Kiki snorted in amusement.

"Are you sure?" Lily whispered.

"Of course," he nodded.

Nodding along with him, Lily let out a calming breath and held out her right hand to him. Was there a motion that was supposed to occur with the wand usually? Using hand movements instead of wand movements did seem to help those spells that specified any. Lily couldn't remember any to go with these spells, though that didn't mean there weren't any.

Oh, she'd just have to go for it!

"*Okesoma Svica*" The stammer in her words caused Oscar's ears to be the only thing that changed and Kiki's laugh to continue.

"You're not helping Ki," Oscar scolded before nodding to Lily again. "You've got this."

Her cheeks red from embarrassment, Lily held out her hand towards Oscar again. She tried again. His face elongated but nothing else. Taking in a deep breath, trying to ignore Kiki who was shaking in her effort not to laugh at the sight, Lily focused harder than she had when trying to direct magic through her 'wand' in the early days.

"*Okesoma Svica!*"

Finally, stood before her was a little black rat with a twitching pink nose and a flesh coloured tail. It chittered up at her before holding up its paw and giving her a congratulatory pat on her knee. It then turned and dashed into the long grass.

"Huh? He can't talk in that form?" Kiki mused, jumping onto Lily's lap and settled down to wait.

"That might work to our advantage, he can't accidentally give himself away."

"True... Hopefully he finds something useful."

"Hopefully I can turn him back." Lily whispered, setting Kiki off into a set of giggles that lasted for some time.

~

Being a rat made the run to the village so much longer than Oscar anticipated! His new legs were so short and his body was so rotund in the middle.

'Great. She made me into a fat rat.'

He thought to himself, pausing in the shadow of the first house he reached to catch his breath. Or perhaps it was just because he was used to being able to take long strides or fly when his legs were tired. Lily would have to learn how to turn him into a bird if they were going to do this again.

Darting under a storage box of wood as feet marched past, he dipped his head out to follow where they were heading. Inside the village was definitely looking like a scene described in history books of war. There were people in uniform everywhere, the locals of the village skirting around them and keeping out of their way. Did they not want them there?

One uniformed woman stopped a child and demanded they hand over the food they were carrying, claiming they were thieving and she would let it go if they just handed it over. When the father of the child walked up to clear up the situation, he was thrown back with a flick of the female's wand.

"How dare you question me, I am Lucretia Byrne, leader of this company! Food delivered here is to handle the hunting effort!" She struck every syllable with cold accuracy. "Could there be a reason you are trying to deter us? Perhaps you are conspiring with the fairies?"

Oscar gasped and ran through the muddy undergrowth to get closer to the scene. A Byrne! Was that someone related to Quintina and Cyrus as well? Perhaps they were someone who could give them information. The female shared the same green eyes that Finnigan had but her hair was a sharp grey colour with stubborn wisps of brown from her original colour.

Hmm, even eternals could go grey?

That was unexpected. Oscar nestled himself into the end of a drainage pipe near the building she was standing in front of and which seemed to have a number of uniformed people entering and exiting.

"The draconians have thrown their hands in with the fairies, hoping to destroy us witches! We are here to stop them. The resources in this village are to help us in the north most stop to the mountains." Lucretia was scolding over the young child who had started crying when their father had fallen to the floor.

So, that was how they were justifying the raid and capture of the tribe. Of course, this would have to be led by a Byrne, any rational person might have thought to do investigation before spreading the fear. But this lady gave the speech freely and strongly as though it was something she truly believed.

How Oscar wanted to bite her... just jump and latch his now huge incisors onto that finger she pointed accusingly at the village members.

"Please, we apologise. My wife is sick and my child just wanted to help." The man finally spoke as he pushed himself to his feet and lifted the bawling child into his arms.

"I'll have medicine sent to your home." A man leaving the building chimed in, gaining a sideways look from Lucretia. "I'm sure we have something that will help."

Oscar focused on the man, he was older than most in uniform and looked almost frail. Was he the physician for the group?

"The medicine is derived from the Lanuvi plant that's only found in the mountains, sir. I'm sure the draconians would burn it before they allowed it to be used on my wife."

Oscar rolled his eyes. Everyone really was blinded by lies and racial hatred. Shaking his head, Oscar decided to dash inside the building while no eyes were on the ground. Scampering up into the rafters of what appeared to be a small tavern, Oscar's beady eyes tried to take in what he could see below, though he wasn't sure he understood it.

Multiple tables had been pulled together in the centre of the room and various pieces of paper appeared scattered over a map of the Xeomont Peaks. Little pins were stuck into the map at different places, one of which Oscar concluded was where Xalina's tribe had been. Were the other pins there because they'd attacked and captured other tribes too? There wouldn't have been many in the mountains, but was Lucretia intending on taking them all into custody under the pretence that they were siding with fairies for the upcoming war?

'It's just going to cause further segregation between everyone', Oscar thought as he ground his teeth in annoyance. Quintina and Cyrus really had the whole thing exactly how they wanted it with fear and distrust keeping everyone in their correct places to continue the plan.

Settling into the rafters, Oscar narrowed his beady eyes to focus on the different discussions and different papers below. From what he could gather, the Draconians were being taken straight past this village and taken south-east towards a big empty area of land with a building in the centre. A prison, perhaps?

"Your spell work is pathetic!" Oscar jumped at the sudden shout, his eyes darting to the commotion between two men. One was towering over the other who didn't look like he wanted to be there. He looked scared, hesitant and almost like he was going to cry under the scrutiny of the older man. "How have I raised such a deplorable excuse for a witch that can't even get his head around the basics of these combat spells!"

The man smacked the youth over the head with a scroll in his hands, gaining whimpered apologies. Oscar felt the defensive tension rise up within him that was similar to how he always felt around Lily. It would seem the witch world was just as demanding in ways that the fairy one was. Though, it was new to find someone who was forcing another into war… Over all the years, fear had become anger at the other races, and that anger didn't seem to tolerate failure.

Shaking his head, Oscar focused on the scroll. Combat spells. That could certainly be useful, even if it just gave them knowledge of what kind of spells might be used against them. Maybe there would even be defensive spells described.

Sifting through the rafters until he was above the raging man, Oscar scratched his ear with his back leg, taking a moment to contemplate if his next action was a wise one. Shrugging to himself, he shifted until he was leaning over the rafter so he could aim himself. Falling onto the man's hand, causing yells of surprise, he sunk his large teeth into the back of the man's hand. The scroll dropped to the floor. While it was rather nice to make a liche like this man flail in the attempt to get Oscar to let go, it wasn't the plan to hold on for long.

Oscar wanted that scroll.

Releasing the man's hand, Oscar fell to the floor ungraciously. Instantly, the man attempted to stamp on him but Oscar was quick to get out of the way and grab the scroll before darting for the front door.

Feet and spells attempted to stop him, but he cleared the front step and scrambled through the people walking in his direction like a salmon swimming against a stream.

Skidding to a halt only when he was safely under the wooden porch of a home, Oscar paused to catch his breath. No one had followed him, which meant they must have either considered him wild or the scroll just not vital enough to get back. Nudging the scroll open with his nose, Oscar scanned the contents with his eyes widening.

Those spells were nothing like what Lily had been learning in Quintegia. These were aggressive, even violent spells. They weren't for forwarding a community, they were for tearing another one down.

Gulping, Oscar rolled the scroll back up and took it into his mouth before heading back out from under the porch. He had to get back to Lily.

~

"So, they DO rip our wings off?!" Lily exclaimed as they studied the scroll Oscar had stolen. They had retreated back towards the mountain so they would be out of sight and Lily had folded broken tree trunks to provide a small barrier in the direction of the village.

"Must be to keep up the illusion..." Kiki snarled

> *'Laceralas - The tearing of wings from the back of an enemy. Use the incantation "Lacera" while brandishing the wand in a large diagonal downward motion.'*

"There's more though, these must be taught solely to those who are going to be in a fight?" Oscar mused. "They don't teach them in Quintegia, unless they have specific fighting schools too?"

"They're all pretty nasty..." Lily murmured as she continued to read the list.

> *'Katanaki - The cutting of solid object in front of you. The cut's direction will be whichever direction the wand is moved. Use the incantation "Katan".*
>
> *Manacht - To take control of another's mind. Need to be close to the recipient and keep a sharp focus in your own mind. If not, it can backfire and they will control yours if they know what they are doing. Use the incantation "Manac".'*

"That must be why the draconians weren't fighting back." Lily concluded aloud. Mind control. "These are horrible..."

There were more; a spell for binding the body completely, one for silencing a voice completely, one for changing objects into daggers... you name it, if it would help with defeating an enemy, it was likely on that scroll.

Every moment that passed the situation they had put themselves in seemed more ominous and hopeless than it had when they had slept the night before.

"How are we ever going to make a difference? I don't want to have to use this kind of thing against others. Most of these people are just doing what they believe is right because they have been lied to for so long…" Lily pulled her knees up to her chest and hugged them tight.

"So, don't use them." Oscar smoothed, nuzzling into her side. "We'll figure out a way to deal with it. Be defensive rather than offensive."

"And how exactly do you want to be defensive against them twisting our limbs until they break?" Kiki demanded, pawing at the scroll where the spell she spoke on sat in writing.

"Yes, how indeed?" A cold voice commented from behind the barrier they had created, making all three of them jump. Immediately, Lily threw her hand out to grab the polearm and pressed it against the manipulated tree trunks and grew them wider and taller to give them more protection. Focused magic was certainly stronger. Though this only received a laugh from the cold voice.

"It's Lucretia…" Oscar hissed. She must have followed him. "I'm sorry!"

Lily shook her head as the tree was slashed in half by a spell from the other side and Lucretia's face appeared in the gap created. Her green eyes filled Lily with fear and misery.

"They have the same eyes…" she mumbled, her heart clenching in her chest.

"Lily!" Kiki yelled as Lucretia lifted her wand. Lily shook her head, dragging herself back to the present and pulled water from the tree trunks, leaving them shrivelled in shape, and shot it up around Lucretia's hand and wand, freezing it instantly.

It wouldn't last. Lucretia was bound to be able to break the ice.

Lily stood for a moment, in the ready stance she had been taught by the draconians with her scythe pointed at her enemy. Could she cut Lucretia down? Her hand trembled. She couldn't do it. She couldn't cross that space and make that move to end a life.

She had to do something.

"*Tikusoma Svica,*" She channelled her focus with the first non-offensive spell that came to mind.

Instantly, Lucretia's wand hit the floor as her body was changed to that of a dormouse.

"Erm... interesting choice?" Kiki chortled as Oscar launched himself through the undergrowth to pounce on the mouse and pick her up in his mouth so she couldn't escape.

"I blanked! I couldn't think of anything but the spells on that stupid scroll!" Lily whined in slight embarrassment.

"Don't knock it," Oscar mumbled around Lucretia's body. "It was a blooming good move."

"True. We now have one Byrne captured and not able to keep scaring people into doing what they want." Kiki laughed as she raised a paw to poke at the little face of Lucretia, swatting her when she attempted to bite.

"What do we do with her?" Lily asked.

"We could eat her?" Kiki suggested.

"She's still a person, Ki."

"So?! She'd kill you given the chance."

"I told you, I don't want to be like that."

Kiki huffed a sigh, glaring at the mouse as though she was contemplating just eating it anyway. However, Lily moved over to the broken trunk and tapped the base of the scythe against it. A small, tight barred cage grew and detached itself.

"Put her in that for now." Lily sighed, shutting the lid of it once Lucretia was dropped in and sealing it with magic. Lucretia immediately started scratching at the wooden bars. Well, that wouldn't work. Chewing her lower lip, Lily debated for a moment. *"Addari."* The barrier spell that had kept her satchel safe all this time made it so those little claws on Lucretia's feet couldn't make contact with the wood. She couldn't scrap her way out.

"I'll try to make sure you aren't like this for too long." Lily promised the little mouse before placing the cage into the satchel along with the scroll of spells.

"You said they were taking the draconians south east?" She turned to Oscar who nodded. "Ok. We'll head that way once we've taken the flowers to that ill woman."

"What?!"

"You want to go into that village?! There's witches who want to capture you everywhere in there!"

Lily turned her eyes to both the cats and her expression was the most annoyed they had ever seen. She understood they were being protective of her, but her mind was made up.

"You said she needed medicine. I'm not just going to walk away from someone who I can help." Yes, she was still naive and idealistic, but she could at least help save one person right now. It was much more achievable than stopping this war it would seem.

"Do you even know what the Lanuvi plant is?" Oscar questioned with a logic Lily couldn't fault.

"No." She admitted. "But there's not many plants that grow there... so I'll just draw them all down to me and take them all."

Oscar let his head fall forward as he laughed softly. "You don't have to do this."

"If I don't, will she die?"

Silence fell over the three of them.

"Then, I do have to do this."

Lily sighed softly and adjusted the satchel on her shoulder and held the scythe with both hands. Slamming the base of it into the ground, Lily closed her eyes and harnessed the power within her body. Focusing it through the scythe, into the ground and back up the mountain, she searched for plant life. Even if it was just a seed, she honed in on it.

"I wonder if anyone else back home knows just how much they could do if they were willing to break the rules and be creative." Oscar mused as he watched a few flowers begin to sprout around Lily's feet. The fact that Lily had to be creative from the start to survive was a blessing now. She was adaptable to any situation and environment she came across.

Once the flowers had bloomed by her feet, Lily pulled the scythe out of the ground and let a yawn wash over her. Today was starting to take its toll. Magic on a large scale appeared to have a knock-on effect on the body; which was news to her. Perhaps that was why she had slept a lot as a child, because she was having to use magic more than any other child in the woodland.

"We should rest before we go," Oscar chimed in. "It's been a long day already. Plus, if we go into the village at night, there should be less people around."

Hopefully.

Lily nodded in agreement. "We have no shelter now though."

"I'll keep watch," Kiki said. "I haven't burned as much energy as you. Plus, I napped while Oscar was in the village."

Agreeing to the idea, Lily walked back to the broken tree trunks which would at least mask them from the view of anyone at a distance. Lying on the ground in the open air was hardly warm, but the clothing from the draconians was more than enough to keep her toasty. So, drawing the coat over her like a blanket and Oscar curled up by her chest, Lily allowed herself to find some uncomfortable sleep.

Chapter 7: Less Fortunate

The village was not as quiet and motionless as they had hoped for the middle of the night. Thankfully, this was hardly her first time sneaking around. Lily did as she knew well, stayed in the shadows and made them deeper and darker so that no one saw her coming. Oscar took the lead, following the scent of the distressed child he had watched earlier until they found the house they resided in.

It was on the outskirts of the village. Run down, smelling of damp, and creaking under the light wind.

"Well, that can't be helping…" Lily mumbled. Damp wouldn't be helping anyone's health, and she was surprised to find that magic hadn't been used to get rid of it.

Pushing the door open, Lily glanced around the darkness. The downstairs was practically bare. This family had next to nothing. Her eyebrows knitted together as she frowned. With magic in the world, how could there be such a difference between the rich city or marble and colour, and this empty home.

"Who's there?!"

A scared voice sounded from the stairs, trembling legs descending them. Lily sighed and placed her scythe against the wall beside the front door.

"Your door was unlocked, I just came to drop off some flowers." Lily spoke, holding up her hands to show one empty and the other holding a small bouquet of flowers. "I heard someone needed flowers from the mountains."

The man was on the ground floor properly now, a lamp ignited to show the image of the intruder which he aimed a long bat at. No wand? Lily noted with mild confusion.

"You!" He exclaimed in fear. "You're that fairy!"

"Yes." Lily confirmed, having not bothered to hide her hair, ears, eyes or shimmer of her skin. "But I'm just here to give you these."

His brown eyes flicked to the flowers and the tension in his arms loosened, the bat lowering in his surprise.

"Lanuvi flowers…" he whispered in disbelief.

"I didn't know which they were, so I got every plant I could find." Lily explained, edging towards the table which sat central to the room and laid the flowers down on them.

"Why?" The man breathed. "You want us dead…" He sounded hesitant about the fact he thought he knew. Lily shook her head softly and smiled sadly.

"I don't want anyone dead." She whispered back to him. "I want to save people from this war, people just don't want to hear that." Nodding her head to him again, she moved towards the door before pausing, curiosity getting the better of her. "Why haven't you used magic to capture me?"

Her silver eyes focused on the man who seemed to flush in embarrassment.

"I, erm… I'm not very good at magic…"

Blink. Blink.

Well that wasn't the answer Lily was expecting.

"But you're a witch?" Kiki piped up.

"Yes." He averted his gaze almost in shame. Lily reached down to nudge Kiki and scold her for the judgment in her voice. Who were they to judge others when they didn't fit the mold? Speaking of, that must be why there was so much dampness in the building.

"Well, allow me to do something else while I'm here then," despite the look of distrust on his face, Lily placed her left hand against the wooden wall and pulled the mould and the water to that spot and drew it out of the wall until there was a ball of it hovering over her hand. "That will help all of your health."

Without another word, she took hold of the scythe with her spare hand and left the house. It didn't seem like he was going to sound an alarm and let everyone know Lily was here, but she also didn't want to risk it when she didn't need to. She had done what she had come into the village to do, and now she and the cats fled the settlement in the silent darkness, each second passing as quiet as the next.

"He's not alerting anyone," Oscar noted obviously.

"Perhaps he won't tell anyone; he'll get into trouble if they find out he did nothing." Kiki murmured, hoping that her prediction was right. If he hadn't called for help back when Lily stood in front of him, he shouldn't be doing so once she was gone.

"Either way, his wife should hopefully recover. Maybe he will start thinking about whether the war is worth it too…" Lily commented as she glanced up to the stars to figure out the direction they were supposed to be going.

"I don't think one low-magic witch is going to turn the tides." Kiki huffed.

"Maybe. But it's something." Lily motioned to the set of stars they needed to be following and started walking, her coat left open to allow the cool air of the evening to get beneath to stop her overheating. "And if enough people start questioning it, then maybe we stand a chance of convincing people to stop."

It still seemed like a too tall order, so silence fell over the three as they travelled.

One foot in front of the other foot.

The mantra was back in her mind as tundra turned to grassland. There was a silent emptiness to the world. Did the witches still think they were up in the mountains? Were more tribes being punished for Lily's very existence? Lily would just have to help them when they found wherever they were all being taken to.

The land they walked through was beautiful, full of wild flowers and the breeze was fresh and freeing. However, after the fourth day of walking in the same direction without a sign of settlement, it was beginning to get tedious.

"How big do you reckon this island is?" Lily sighed as they stopped for lunch, it being much easier to grow enough food now there were plants aplenty.

"I have a feeling we're the only ones that even have a taste of the size, so who knows." Oscar chortled, keeping an eye on Lucretia who had been taken out of the satchel so Lily could put food in for her in her mouse form.

A crunch sounded nearby to where they were seated hidden in long grass making them all freeze.

"Someone's here!" Kiki hissed urgently, Lily unceremoniously stuffing Lucretia's cage back into the satchel. Lily lowered herself to the ground, though froze upon the sound of a familiar feminine voice.

"Lily? You out here?"

Without thought, Lily stood and found herself looking across the grass and flowers at the auburn curly hair she knew so well.

"Dia?" She breathed, not daring to believe her eyes. Why was Dia here? Worse, why was she pointing her wand at Lily? Did she really believe that Lily was a villain who had used her? Leaving the scythe on the floor, Lily raised her hands in front of her just like she had done at the ill witch's house. She didn't want to fight Dia.

As she had stood, heartache shone in Dia's eyes as though she hadn't believed that Lily would really be there. "So, it's true?"

"What's true?"

"Everything you told me was a lie." Dia motioned at all of Lily, finally seeing her in her true colours. Her eyes even flicked to the pointed ends of Lily's ears that were visible with her hair behind them.

"Not everything…" Lily sighed.

"Oh yeah? So, you weren't in the school to get information on us witches and you didn't befriend me to make it easier?" Dia spat angrily. Lily faltered, because initially that was exactly what happened.

"It's true that you were my first ever friend." Lily started. "And that you made me rethink everything I have ever been taught! This whole war is pointless, Dia. Please, you have to believe me!"

"Oh, I do, do I?" Dia rolled her eyes. "You've done nothing but lie. I suppose you aren't currently travelling through our lands looking for weaknesses for your armies either?"

"I was banished from my home!" Lily yelled over Dia's accusations, cutting off her voice and glaring at the auburn-haired girl with both frustration and desperation. "I have nowhere left to go. I can never see my parents again. I lost you and Tanith. Finnigan broke my heart. I'm traipsing across this whole land because, even though I lost you all, I don't want you to die. I want to stop this stupid war! Both sides are wrong in their reasons to be defensive. Fairies don't want your land. And witches don't want to collect wings from dead fairies! This war doesn't need to happen! But no one will listen!"

Her hands had fallen to her sides and balled up into fists as she let the frustration flow from her lips. Why was everyone so blind?! At her feet, Oscar and Kiki moved in closer to give her some emotional support if they could. Lily hadn't lost them, they wouldn't let her forget that. She was never alone with them around.

As her breath slowed, Lily's silver eyebrows drew together at a sudden thought.

"Dia... why are you here?" This was a long way from the school and the town next door where Dia lived with her father.

The distrust on Dia's face had already been waning, but now a flicker of fear shot across her eyes. "I have to make up for my mistake." Her hand trembled a little as she pointed her wand at Lily once more. "I fell for all your lies and now I need to make up for it."

Lily frowned, edging a little closer to the one she still called her best friend. "Dia? What happened after the alarm was put out for me?"

Dia's eyes widened a little as they began to water. As she stepped closer, Lily could see there was bruising on Dia's arms and a couple of scars by her lip where it had been split. What told most, however, was the raised red tattoo on the side of her neck spelling out 'failure'. Without care, Lily closed the space between them and threw her arms around Dia in a tight hug, ignoring the wand that jabbed into her chest. Lily had had her suspicions that Dia's father didn't always give her a choice in tattoos and wasn't the most pleasant of people. Anytime he had been spoken off was short and distant from Dia, or filled with an excuse and nervous laughter.

As soon as arms were around her, Dia burst into tears. Lily wasn't sure if Dia believed her, but right now, that didn't actually matter.

"I have to catch you, Lil." Dia sobbed into Lily's shoulder, the sound of fearful defeat breaking Lily's heart even more than Finnigan had managed. "He'll do worse if he finds out I found you and didn't catch you."

Lily tightened her arms around Dia, trying to give her support and safety while she let out the pain she had likely hidden from everyone but the silence of the night with nothing but a pillow for comfort. The cats had hopped up to hover close to try and offer their own support, Kiki nuzzled at Dia's visible cheek to wipe away the tears while Oscar settled near her back and began to purr soothingly.

"I should have known these two were too smart to be normal witch companions." Dia laughed pitifully.

Lily pulled back from the hug and tenderly lifted her right hand to place her fingers to the vicious tattoo. Closing her eyes, she focused on the water molecules used in the ink. It was early enough that the skin wasn't stained with the pigment yet, and so, she was able to move the ink and change the shape to a majestic wing with a few feathers falling from it.

"You can take me in," She said as she lowered her hand.

"What?!" Oscar and Kiki yelped, though Lily raised a hand to quiet them. Lily would escape… or she wouldn't. Either way, she couldn't let Dia suffer if she could help it.

"It's ok," Lily brushed the tears off Dia's confused face. "I'm not going to fight you. And I'm not going to run knowing you'll be hurt if I do."

"Lil…"

"I just want you to consider that maybe I'm telling you the truth; fairies aren't your enemy; the whole thing is a lie." Leaning forward to press a kiss to Dia's forehead, a comforting gesture that Lily's mother used to give her when she was having a rough day. Stepping back to pick up the scythe from the floor, Lily handed it over to Dia. "I'm now disarmed."

"You can use magic without a wand and you know it." Dia half chuckled as she shook her head. Lily smiled lightly and shrugged. "Are you sure…?" Dia hesitated, raising her wand once more.

"I'm surer of this than I've been of anything else I've done in months." There wasn't a single doubt in her mind about this choice.

"Thank you," Dia whispered before muttering the sleeping spell at firing it straight at Lily's head rendering her asleep before her body even hit the floor.

An uncomfortable strain pulled on her shoulder joints, dragging her back to consciousness after the spell had worn off. There was no force on any part of her body apart from her wrists which felt like they were being dragged skyward.

Opening her eyes, Lily realised that it was the rest of her being pulled down by gravity, but rope bound around her wrists stopped her from falling. Narrowing her eyes lethargically, she attempted to focus on what was happening. The rope holding her was tied to the front of a broomstick under the hands of the rider. In front of them were a few more broomsticks, each carrying their own bound captive. Lily could see Kiki and Oscar bound by their paws under a broom two places in front of her. She couldn't reach them from here, and from their lack of movement, they were still asleep. Other captives were draconian and witch by the looks of things. She must be on her way to the place they were locking everyone up.

Not that she would be able to do much if she was a bound captive herself.

Wait... bound...

Her head snapped upwards to focus on her wrists. They were encased in the magic-inhibiting metal she had experienced before, except these weren't burning her skin. Glancing at the rider of the broomstick to make sure they hadn't realised she was conscious, Lily pulled herself up with effort to gain a closer look at her wrists. No matter which way her body was shifted with the movements of the broom, the metal never touched her skin. There was a gap that never got crossed. Had Dia cast a protection spell around Lily's wrists? Could she be hopeful that maybe her friend wasn't completely against her?

Whether Dia was on her side or just had a moment of doubt didn't matter; she had given Lily an opportunity.

"*Agora!*" She cupped her hands around the rope and set the fibres alight.

"Hey! What?!" The witch above yelled, but it was already too late. The rope snapped and Lily dropped to the ground, creating steps of ice to jump from in stages so she didn't just crash to the floor and do more damage to her ankle.

The ground she landed on was a deserted field that spanned as far as the eye could see. It was filled with cracks and crevices, and it appeared that not a single plant aside from orange hued grass grew there. Stranger still, despite the cursing and yelling of the witches above, none of them chased her to the ground.

"You are an absolute failure."

Lily spun around at the voice to find her face-to-face with herself.

Chapter 8: Voices

"What?" Lily breathed.

The image of herself was blurred at the edges and the eyes were a darker grey compared to her silver, it's expression harsh and judgmental. But, it was definitely her.

Reaching out a hand, she found that her arm moved straight through the image and it dispersed into thin air.

"What was that?" Lily frowned. Shaking her head, she glanced up to the sky to determine which way they were travelling. Now she had to get Oscar and Kiki back along with Tanith and Xalina.

Struggling with the metal cuffs, Lily grumbled at them before sealing ice around them and freezing them until the joints cracked and broke.

"You're so pathetic."

Lily's image was back, looking at her with disgust. Lily couldn't describe just how unnerving it was to be watched by your own eyes, but it wasn't something she enjoyed at all. Waving her arm through the image it vanished again. Had one of the witches cast some spell on her when she had been falling? Perhaps one that made her see things? Shrugging it off, she had more important things to worry about than images that weren't real.

Taking a step in the direction the witches had been carrying them, another image appeared.

"I'm so disappointed in you." Her mother looked at her with betrayal in her eyes. "How could you choose witches over your own family?"

Another wave of her arm made that vanish too.

It wasn't true, she hadn't chosen anyone over anyone else. She was just trying to help. Just trying to save those she loved.

"I should never have helped you escape…" her father's voice made her spin around to face his image.

"You'd never say that." Lily stated firmly before dismissing that image as well.

Was this really a spell? Surely the caster would need to be close to keep it going.

Stepping over a larger crack in the ground, her face appeared again. Every step, another face, another comment, another criticism. They cycled through faces who had always criticised her.

"Useless."

"Freak."

"Abomination."

They also started to provide unwanted advice and conclusions.

"Just give up."

"Nobody wants you."

"Accept your death."

"No one will help you."

"No one will save you."

"No one could love you."

Dealing with those faces was achievable, Lily had been doing it all her life. Even if she believed them, it did not stop her from taking the next step.

It was whenever her parents' images appeared that she faltered. When Jared appeared with a sneer telling her how much just being nice to her had ruined his life. He told her of all the consequences he faced from his mother and how it was all Lily's fault. Her parents told her how they were outcasted by their kind as well and it was Lily's fault.

The only time the images stopped showing up was when Lily's movements stopped.

Lying on the ground, hours after first steps over the cracked ground, she found silence... but it wasn't the peaceful silence everyone wanted. The world around her was silent, but the phrases and the echoes of the images repeated in her mind over and over.

"It's not real," she muttered to no one as she covered her head in her arms and curled up into a tight foetal position as if that would protect her.

The images and voices continued for days.

Lily wasn't sure how many, but she knew she had slept at least twenty times by the time she really started to feel grated by the words.

Every time she grew some food or drew water from the ground to survive, she was plagued by a barrage of voices telling her not to bother, or that the food was poison, or that she should just turn around and lock herself up for good. Every step she took she was reminded of her failures, of how pathetic she was and how unwanted she was by every fairy in her past.

"Shut up," she whimpered after her mother had told her just how terrible it had been birthing an abomination. "I'm a good person."

"Liar." The new voice caused Lily to freeze in her steps forward, steps which had steadily gotten more shaken and considerably slower. Dia scowled at her on her left. "Because of you, I have my failure etched onto my skin."

"You've destroyed our lives!" Xalina appeared to the right. "We're all going to die and it's because of you."

"We were supposed to be your friends." Tanith appeared beside Xalina. All of them were scratched up and beat down, bruised and bloodied by the effects Lily had brought into their lives.

"No…" Lily shook her head, stumbling backwards and drawing up the images and voices of her parents again.

"Stop. I'm not…" Not what? She was a failure. She was the reason Dia had been hurt. She was the reason Xalina and her people had been raided and captured. She was the reason Oscar and Kiki were now locked up. How could she know that her parents weren't suffering punishment because of Lily's escape? Perhaps they too would come to hate her for the pain she had caused.

"I just want to help…" tears brimmed her eyes and clung to her pale eyelashes.

"Stupid."

"Idiot."

"Fool."

Lily stopped her movements to make the voices vanish. Only when silence hit her ears and ringing echoed in her mind did she allow those tears to fall to her cheeks. She didn't want to take another step. She didn't want to hear anymore. Every day the scenery stayed the same. It was a barren, cracked wasteland that she was stuck in. It seemed endless.

Sitting on the ground and glancing up at the fading light of the day's sky, Lily attempted to calm the tears. She didn't even know if she was still going in the right direction. How could you see as far as the horizon and yet feel completely trapped? The moment she stood up and took another step those voices would be back. Though who would it be next? Herself, her friends, her family... all options were enough to make her curl up on the floor in the attempt to rest again.

Every time period between sleep was getting shorter. Each day she could cope with less. After several more sunsets, she walked with a stumble, arms waving in front of her with every step to try and counter the ghosts of her anxiety.

"You can't succeed."

"You're just a child."

"You've abandoned us."

"I hate you."

"You'll never be loved."

"Shut up... shut up!" Lily mumbled breathlessly. Her tears had dried up. How many days had gone by since that had happened? When had her tears given way to hopelessness in her silver eyes? The voices were right. They had to be. They echoed even when they weren't there. They etched themselves onto her mind and brain. She had failed.

"Bring her back!" The young female draconian whose mother died. "Why did you have to come here?!"

Lily wobbled as she moved past the girl. She had definitely failed that little girl in particular.

"And any other draconian who lost someone that day," she reminded herself out loud.

"If you hadn't come to us, we would still be safe." The face of the Dregana hissed at her.

"I know."

"Tanith will be tried as a traitor now they know she was with us." Xalina spat. "It'll be your fault if she dies!"

"I know."

"We'll die before the war because you couldn't keep to yourself."

"I'm sorry."

Swaying on the spot, Lily glanced around at the empty world. Her head throbbed with pain from the continuous screaming in her mind. She was sorry. Maybe she should stop. If she laid down here and never got up again then no one else could be hurt by her actions. The voices would stay only inside her head until darkness finally came to take her. She would truly be able to find peace and perfect silence.

She would be free.

Free of criticism. Free of the pain. Free of the heartbreak.

"Breaking you really is too easy."

Lily opened her eyes to look into the green ones which made her heart leap and seize at the same time. Finnigan smirked at her, his face so close to hers that their noses could almost touch. He whispered to her, his voice the quietest so far, and yet, they stabbed deeper still. "How you could ever think I could love you is beyond me? I mean, come on. You're pathetic. You cry all the time. You are deformed. You fit in nowhere. You are weak, pathetic and frankly you look weird. As if someone like me could ever hold a flame for you…"

Lily sighed and hung her head where she stood. Finnigan still plagued her dreams, seeing him while awake as well was enough to make her stomach turn.

"Leave me alone." She grumbled, waving her hand through his body and attempting to walk away. His body vanished for a moment and then reappeared in front of her again.

"I'll always be with you, Lil." His voice was venomously sweet. "I took your heart. I am the reason you know what it's like to be bound and powerless. And I still have your heart, don't I?" His hand reached out and moved through her chest where her heart was.

"No, you don't."

"Oh yes I do. Otherwise you wouldn't have hope that I'm not that bad because I couldn't kill you. You wouldn't dream about me. My face and voice wouldn't hurt you so much."

"I don't love you."

"Yes... you do." Finnigan vanished again as she slashed her arm through his body.

"No, I don't. If anything, I hate you." Lily snarled, anger and misery twisting together like an ugly parasite that wanted to control her body. She could feel the warmth of her blood rushing under her skin.

"No. You hate yourself." He retorted, appearing behind her with a dark laugh. "You hate yourself because you know I'm always going to own part of you."

"Shut up!" Lily yelled, stamping her foot through the legs of the image, creating a seismic shockwave as her foot hit the ground. Dust and rocks shook over the ground for as far as she could see and Finnigan's image vanished. The ground continued to tremor, crevices altering in size at the movement of earth.

"Did I just..." Lily glanced to her foot with a degree of surprise mixing into the angry pain on her face. That was the *Sokaruu* spell, the same she had used to create the avalanche to escape Finnigan. This time though, she hadn't uttered the spell.

Had she just managed witch magic without verbal command... Was that even possible?

"Right. That's enough." She growled to herself, taking a step forward and immediately banishing the figure that appeared with water pulled from the ground and moulded into three floating daggers of ice hovering around her body.

Each step was fuelled by anger, even the slightest of movement or sound triggered her hand flicking to guide an ice shard through the image. Prickled plants began to grow by her feet each time one connected to the floor, the growing anger in her mind fuelling them to grow larger and in unpredictable shapes. The orange grass she walked past became scorched while shadows grew around her despite the high sun.

"I will save them." She commented to herself, slashing another image down that reminded her she was weak. She had to do something to prove to herself that all these voices weren't right. Desperate for something to like about herself, she pushed on; her magic spilling over in the environment around her helping silence the voices and images quickly. "I have to save them."

The new mantra kept her going until she finally caught sight of a large building in the distance.

"You'll get them all killed." Dia sighed before vanishing with a violent swipe of a thorny branch.

"Shut up." Lily had no idea what her plan was, but she would not allow them to die. She wouldn't. She couldn't. Lily didn't care how much her body was shaking from the effort of her journey, she would make her legs move whether they wanted to or not.

By the time she could see detail on the structure, the alarm had been sounded and she could see figures standing in windows and around the entrance to the right.

The voices had become constant whispers now, even without images to go with them.

There was so much noise.

Even without the cries of the witches yelling about defence, Lily felt deafened by the sensation.

Flicking her head and hair to try and get rid of the voices, she looked like she had gained a violent twitch.

Drawing water from the ground and the plants growing by her feet, Lily created an ice shielded to her right side and above as spells were sent her way. They chipped at the ice which just replenished itself.

"Pathetic."

"Weak."

Growling at the voices she reached the side of the building and slammed her hand against it. "I'll show you weak." Another shockwave rippled from her palm and through the structure, loosening the large stones which were stacked tight and secure.

Vines and ice took advantage of the gaps that were created, pulling the stones apart and filling them with windows of ice which Lily would be able to get through but others couldn't destroy without threatening the stability of the enlarged structure. As if to prove this, Lily glanced at the witches who ran around the side of the structure to confront her and opened up a hole in the ice window in front of her, stepping through and sealing it behind her.

Chapter 9: Crime of Treason

The building was full of a chill that Lily could laugh in the face of, cold stone and shadow. The infrequency of windows made the place feel indefinitely like a jail with no escape. Though, Lily supposed that was the whole point.

Looking up and down the corridor she had entered, she could see cells bending around each curve on the inner walls.

"Help us!"

"Let us out!"

"Oi! Over here!"

Voices of inmates echoed, almost covering the sound of footsteps running her way. Shifting her right foot in the direction of those approaching, the vines and branches shot out from the frame they were giving the building and sped down the corridor to bind anyone they found.

With the anger in her heart making her expression cold, Lily walked past the closed cells and ventured until she found the witches who were trying to defend the jail.

"Argh. Let us go!"

"Don't kill us!"

Lily's eyes narrowed at the pleading one of the men made for their lives. Each witch was bound with their wand hand wrapped up completely so their wands had fallen to the ground. With a flick of her hand, vines wrapped around their mouths to keep them from speaking. It wasn't unheard of for them to use wandless magic, but they still needed incantations.

"I'm not going to kill anyone." Lily sighed as she walked past them and continued through the corridor looking for Oscar and Kiki. Pausing by the last bound witch, she turned her cold eyes to the female and raised an eyebrow. "Where are my cats?" Even though she was still muffled around the mouth, the way the brown eyes flicked downwards told Lily all she needed to know.

Lily was a force to be reckoned with as she followed the staircases down into the floors below ground level. Anyone who came against her either became bound by vines or sealed to the spot by ice. Every single one had their wand taken and their mouths covered to stop any noise.

"*Dhula!*" The door at the base of the stairs disintegrated to dust as Lily knocked the scythe against it and spoke the incantation. She hadn't been able to master the spell on many materials, but wood was something she knew intimately down to the base molecules.

"Whoa! Hang on!" The male behind a desk yelped before being bound like his colleagues on the upper floors.

"Should make your doors out of metal." Lily mumbled as she walked past into the odd collection of arms obviously taken from those who had been arrested. Wands, polearms, armour... all sorts existed in there, soul companions locked in cages away from their humanoid counterparts.

"Lil!"

Rushing over to the two little cages where Oscar and Kiki jumped up at the bars to try and reach her, Lily felt some of the pain and anger loosen in her heart. They were ok! Kiki has a small cut on her right cheek but otherwise both were completely intact.

"Oh, thank the wings. You're both ok."

"Don't worry about us! Are you ok?"

"Yeah, it took you ages to get here! Did something happen?"

Lily paused in her freezing of the locks to shatter them open. "What do you mean?"

"It's been a month," Oscar explained. "We thought you'd gotten into trouble. Especially when Finnigan turned up here and his stoat came in to mock us."

A month? It had taken her that long to walk a large field? She'd been alone with the voices for that long? All the days had merged together, and she had definitely laid down more regularly to sleep in silence where it was safe from torment more than she should have.

"I'm sorry." She whispered shamefully as the locks cracked open on all cages. The companions quickly dashed out their confines and out the door to find their counterparts.

"Don't be sorry," Oscar jumped up onto her lap and nuzzled against her cheek while Kiki hopped up onto Lily's shoulder and purred loudly. "What happened?"

Lily lowered her gaze before catching them up; it was sickening to have to repeat half of the things that continued to repeat in her mind even though the voices were gone. But they'd kept up with her as she walked that route for a month! So, maybe they were right.

Maybe she was pathetic and everything she was trying to do was pointless.

"That makes sense." Oscar commented when she had finished. "We heard the witches talk about how no one ever escapes here because of the cursed land surrounding it. Anyone who steps foot on it will be put through torture of the mind."

"Yeah, it's why they tag the wings of fairies and draconians that get put in here," Kiki added with a venomous tone. "Makes the wings so heavy that they can't fly."

"Welcome to my world…" Lily mumbled with a shrug. "We'll have to remove the tags so people can escape." Pushing herself to her feet, Lily walked back over to the desk the witch was still bound behind. Further past him was a storage unit filled with files.

Turning back to the witch she raised an eyebrow. "Is there a list of who is in what cell and what they did?" She had a lack of patience about her which showed through the appearance of crackling ice in the air around her. The terror on the witch's face was not something Lily felt good about, but she also found she didn't really care at that moment. If Finnigan was here or nearby, then Lily didn't have time to waste. He may not have killed her last time, but she didn't think she could afford more injuries like her arm.

Glancing to the healing area which remained reddened and stitched together, she shook her head. No, she could do this.

"Tell me." She commanded, pulling the vines away from the male's mouth so he could answer her.

"Drawer on the bottom left! Please don't hurt me... I'm just a record keeper!" The man pleaded. It was wrong to have people so scared of her, she was barely five foot five and she was only sixteen... yet he trembled as his eyes flicked from her face to the shards of ice hovering around her.

Rolling her eyes, she moved the vine back to stop him talking. "I'm not going to hurt you. I'm just here to free those who don't deserve to be here."

"You're going to free more than the draconians?" Kiki asked, hopping up onto the desk.

"You want me to leave fairies and innocent witches behind?" Lily deadpanned.

"Good point." Kiki nodded before leaping back onto the floor and trotting to the door. "Let's bust this place!"

"You're in a good mood," Oscar chortled as Lily pulled the binder from the drawer she had been pointed towards.

"Just excited to see the sun," Kiki chimed, jumping over the wood dust on the floor so as not to dirty her white feet. Lily shook her head, the cat could just fly, but she supposed it was a habit that she still didn't, even though their world had changed considerably.

"Well, we've got quite a few floors to get through first." Lily commented, flicking through the paper in the binder, each page's colouring indicating how long that particular inmate had been there. Frowning at one page that looked almost as old as the parchment in her satchel, she raised an eyebrow. No name, in for treason, no one except the guard captain was allowed into the isolation room where the person was kept. Flicking through she also noted that every inmate was in for treason. Was this where they put anyone who had questioned the world order around them?

"People!" Oscar called as footsteps sounded from the higher floors.

"Not a problem…" Lily placed a hand against the closest wall and reconnected with the vines infecting the building. Shouts of surprise and anger sounded before only prisoner yells for release were left. The cats turned to look at Lily with surprise on their faces, she shrugged in the face of it and stepped out of the records room. "I've had enough."

Walking past any witch she had bound, Lily shattered their wands and continued to the first cell. Shattering the lock with ice, Lily pulled the door open and took in the inmate. They were a light fairy, male, obviously having been there for a while from the outgrown shaggy locks framing his face. His golden eyes were dull and he seemed resigned to the cell even now the door was open. True to Kiki's words, his wings had been tagged together so they couldn't spread and be used to fly.

"Why are you here?" Lily asked, wanting to confirm her theory of the reality of the crime 'treason'.

The man looked at her suspiciously, unsurprising as she had fairy colours but no wings. But Lily kept her feet firm and folded her arms waiting for an answer.

"My friends and I started a protest against the war… next thing we know we're being taken from our homes and locked up in this place." He spat.

"You're against the war?"

"I was... then witches locked me in here."

"Fairies would have had to snatch you from your bed."

"So?!"

Lily sighed. "So... the war is a load of rubbish, it should be stopped. There's corruption in both communities and it's killing so many. If I release you and your friends, I want you to go home and remember that the enemy isn't that clear. Most witches are innocent too."

The man snorted.

"We could just leave you here." Kiki commented coldly from the bars she looked through.

His golden eyes flicked to the two cats before returning to Lily. "Why don't you have wings?"

"Born without them. What?" Lily raised an eyebrow at the sceptical look she was given. "You think I'd have winged, talking companions if I wasn't really a fairy?"

"You're avoiding the deal." Kiki growled, flicking her wings and flying up to mere inches in front of the man's face. "If we let you go, you go home and take up your old viewpoint."

For a moment Lily thought he was actually going to refuse. Though, it didn't really matter, she just wanted to put the cats among the pigeons with people thinking differently when back in their original homes.

"Fine!" The man eventually conceded. "I don't like it, but you're right; innocents don't need to die for stupid wars. But I'm not doing anything to get myself arrested, I don't owe anyone anything."

"You'll owe Lil!" Oscar hissed from the doorway.

"It doesn't matter," Lily interjected calmly. Walking over to the male, she crouched down behind him to get a look at the tag binding his wings. "I don't need anyone to owe me." Grimacing as she examined the tag, she noted that it had teeth which punctured through the wings and linked together to prevent removal without ripping the wings completely.

"Oz, go scout for some keys for these, I don't want to risk using magic and damage the wings more. It'll be uncomfortable enough to fly with these holes in them." Lily called over to the cat still sitting in the doorway. With a nod, he vanished back down the corridor to search the staff who were still bound.

"You know the cavalry will be on their way with that alarm going off?" The male droned with judgment in his voice.

"I'm aware."

"So why aren't you rushing?"

"The whole building is encased in ice and vines that will replenish and give them a hard time."

"Encased??" The man exclaimed angrily. "How are we supposed to escape?"

"When I tell you to." Lily snapped, ice cracking around her feet and rising up in sharp stalagmites. "When you are untagged, you will go and stay next to a bound guard and when I release this building, you will take them and you will fly to safety and leave them somewhere safe."

"But..."

"Enough! These are my terms, if you want to deny me, I'll leave the blooming tag on you." Why couldn't people just do what was right?! The guards were just doing their jobs and she had taken their wands. Doing their jobs was not enough of a crime to have them walk through the nightmare that Lily had experienced firsthand. What if they stopped walking? What if they gave into the voices?

No, Lily was angry at the world but she wasn't cruel.

"I'll let you think it over..." she mumbled as Oscar joined them with a chain of keys dangling from his jaw. Reaching down to take them, Lily left the man in his cell, door open, and moved onto the next one. She'd let him go either way, but she was done being silenced because someone was too blind to see a different viewpoint.

She came up against similar concerns in the cells as she raised through the building. Thankfully, most of the inmates seemed to care more about the freedom than the terms she was putting down. Draconians and fairies agreed to carry the wingless to safety, most fetching one and bringing them back to the cells where Lily had said she would shatter a hole when the time came to escape.

"Lily?!"

"Oly Moly! Girl you are insane!" Tanith yelled as she spotted Lily down the hallway her and Xalina were kept in. "What are you doing here?"

"Sightseeing..." Lily deadpanned, making her way along the corridor, unlocking and de-tagging draconians as she went.

"She's here to rescue you, obviously!" Kiki chimed before announcing the plan for escape to the corridor for everyone to hear, her high-pitched voice cutting through the excitable murmuring of escape.

A ricocheting bang sounded, shaking the whole building and cutting the little cat off.

"Cavalry's here." Oscar stated.

"Took their time." Kiki laughed, "We're most of the way through this place."

"Yeah, but we aren't finished yet. Oz, take this key and go de-tag the stubborn ones." Lily leant down to offer one of the key chains to the larger cat who ran off as soon as he had it gripped. Turning to Xalina, Lily smiled lightly.

"You'll have to carry Tanith out of here. Do not step on the ground below."

"Wait!" Tanith exclaimed, grabbing Lily's elbow as she turned to the stairs "What about you?"

Lily blinked. She hadn't thought about that. Shrugging lightly, she offered an unsure smile "Someone upstairs will carry me I'm sure. The rest of you, spread out along the corridors and if you see a wingless person, pair up with them and get ready to fly!"

The crashing of spells into the ice and vines cocooning the building became almost rhythmic as Lily hurried her way through the last two floors of cells. Debris began to drift to the floor as the building struggled under the onslaught.

"We're going to have to go…" Kiki murmured.

"We will. There's only this floor left." Dodging a larger piece of stone which fell from above, Lily pushed open the door to the final floor.

This floor was different. It was one big room, and in the centre was a large white feline with black stripes designed into its thick fur. The creature was on its chunky paws with its blue eyes narrowed at the turmoil of the building. It had cuffs that bound around the paws to prevent claws being used and it was muzzled tightly. Wind howled through the room, flicking Lily's hair in front of her face the moment she walked in.

"Ok, so we can go?" Kiki commented.

"It'll die if we leave it bound while the building collapses." Lily mused, stepping against the wind to move towards the creature with her hands out to show she wasn't here to harm it. She left her scythe at the doorway and crouched herself down so she was at eye level with the creature. It watched her closely and something in those baby blue eyes made Lily feel like it knew what she was doing. Perhaps it was magical, was that why it was in a prison? The wind died down a little as she reached out her hand to the shackles around its paw. "It's ok…" she soothed. Another thud shook the building, cracking the ceiling above. They didn't have time for her to be going this slowly!

Letting out a huff of breath Lily shattered the hinges of the shackles and unbuckled the muzzle to allow it to fall to the floor.

"Ok. Now we can go."

"How?! We can't fly and that's not got wings!" Kiki yelled over the crumbling sound that indicated the building was reaching its last straw even with the supports Lily held in place.

"I don't know! Everyone else first, then I'll figure something out!"

Lily took hold of the scythe and stood with it in front of her, blade to the floor and slashed into the grout. With the use of the vines now etched throughout the building, Lily punched holes in the sides giving those inside obvious ways to leave so long as they could fly. All she had to do was hope that they did take the wingless.

The structural integrity of the building was officially diminished, Kiki jumped into the air as the floor began to crumble beneath them.

"Get outside!" Lily yelled at the little cat, diving to the side to dodge a large chunk of ceiling. She could hear the faint cries of fighting outside and the snarling of the large cat before her.

"I'm not going to leave you!"

"I can't save everyone Kiki! Get yourself out!" Lily yelled back, eyes desperate as she pulled her scythe out of the floor, jumping away as the area crumbled too. A deep growl sounded and within an instant, Lily was shoved to the floor face first, her grip tightening on her scythe with intent to fight back. However, the feline didn't bite her, instead it took a mouthful of her clothing and leapt up out of the hole in the ceiling and jumped up a few feet in thin air.

Lily blinked, her mind frozen with surprise.

With no wings, this cat was walking… on air…?

A spell shot up and sliced across the cat's nose, causing Lily to be dropped and fall towards the collapsing building. Multiple times her body seemed to get stopped by an invisible force that couldn't quite hold her, turning her stomach and making her hold back vomit when her body finally stopped moving about three feet from the floor.

"How did she...?"

"Who cares! Get her!" That voice. That intoxicatingly painful voice. Lily scrambled to get her feet beneath her to draw up a shroud of shadow around her, watching the confusion of many before her but those green eyes of Finnigan continued to look straight at her. Could he see through the darkness she created? No. That was impossible. Only the caster could see through fairy darkness. Silently pulling up vines from the ground, Lily quickly counted how many were there.

Too many. They were all on charmed tools so they didn't have to step on the ground but thankfully quite a few were aiming at the other escapees.

"*Mariatio.*"

"*Havatu.*"

"*Sokari.*"

An array of spells was launched her way and within the darkness, Lily could do little but attempt to deflect or block. How was she going to get out of this one?

Fire burned through the darkness, licking across the left side of her head, pulling a howl of pain from her throat. Water immediately doused the burn, but not swiftly enough to prevent the hair from being lost from the left side of her head.

Expanding the darkness with her as her body was blown backwards by a *Sokaruu* charm, she glanced around desperate for a way out. Raising a hand to attempt to cradle the wound on her head, she didn't know what to do. She couldn't fly out without being right in the firing range of those spells. The only reason she could block enough now was because they couldn't see her to aim.

Something heavy thudded to the ground behind her, causing her to jump and spin on her heels.

The striped feline.

It sniffed at the air and walked towards her, nudging at her knees and motioning for her to climb on its back, which stood up to her shoulders.

"Yes!" She whispered. "Good plan. You run us out of here and I'll use magic to block their attacks!" Whatever this creature was, it wasn't average but it was certainly going to be the only reason she survived this if she managed to. The creature huffed in a way that sounded like laughter and shook its mighty head as Lily climbed onto its back and held on with her left hand leaving her right with the scythe raised and ready.

The air around them began to pick up in speed, circling around the feline's feet and instantly blasting outwards when it leapt into the air and took a steep path to try and stay ahead of the witches who turned to follow.

The fight was overwhelming immediately.

Spells of all levels of viciousness were sent after her, Lily only being able to block with ice which smashed and broke with every hit. Her eyes closed for a moment as she expected the knife launched her way to hit her. A loud clang made her flinch.

"Lil! You ok?!"

Opening her eyes, Lily couldn't help but smile at the sight of Xalina carrying Tanith while the brunette brandished a long metal pole which looked like she'd torn a prison bar free from the rest.

"What in wings name is that?!" Xalina called, motioning to the feline.

"No idea! But it can walk on air and it's helping!"

"Good enough for me!" Tanith laughed before slashing the pole through the air angrily, attempting to send spells back in return and failing.

"They'll follow us the whole way home!" Xalina curved her wings around Tanith to block a slashing spell sent at them.

"No," Kiki called as she flew over to them. "Oscar just confirmed that the others are retreating back to help these guys. Lil, you're the main target."

"Of course, I am..." Lily rolled her eyes before yelping in surprise as the feline suddenly hissed and spun around to face the witches. They had scorched its back leg with a fire spell, and it returned the favour by roaring and creating a hurricane force wind that knocked all oncoming attackers off course and spiralling to the floor.

"Whoa!" Tanith whistled. "I definitely like this cat!"

"Lil! Move!" Oscar's voice yelled. Turning to find the cat and what he was talking about, Lily saw a flash of silver hurtling her way, then a blur of black which collided with her chest.

"Oz? Oscar!" Lily's jubilation from the sight of spiralling witches was replaced with terror as her mind registered what she held in her arm.

Oscar's body was limp. A large dagger lodged into his side, blood dripping onto the fur beneath them.

Chapter 10: Grief Destroys

"Oscar, stay with me!"

"Oscar!"

"Oh, come on, please. Don't leave me."

Lily and Kiki pleaded to any power in the world until they landed on solid ground and Lily could jump down from the strange feline to examine Oscar closer. He was still, his breathing shallow and his eyes closed.

"Ozzy, wake up. Come on." Lily threw her coat on the ground and laid Oscar carefully on it while nudging his cheek. Kiki tried tugging at his ear with her teeth, a high whine leaving her throat.

Nothing. Not even a twitch of a whisker.

"Oz... please..." Lily choked on the tears spilling over onto her cheeks. He couldn't leave her here. She needed him.

Looking up at Xalina and Tanith who had landed nearby, Lily didn't even have to speak for it to be clear she was pleading for help.

Neither moved. The expressions they wore were ones of sympathy and pain.

"No." Lily denied their acceptance. "No!" Pulling the knife from the cat's body, she attempted to suture the wound together but, with her shaking hands and unstable mind, only a few stitches held. Her right hand was covered in the blood she was trying to stem, while her left hand continued to shake the feline body trying to wake him.

A ripping pain spread through her entire body in an instant. As though someone was dragging a hook straight through her torso and wrenching her heart out in the process. It was torturous enough that the burn on her head seemed numb in comparison.

"Lil... he's not breathing." Kiki whimpered. Lily knew though, that pain had been the connection to his soul dying with him.

Curling herself over the two cats, Lily's body trembled with pain and sorrow. Oscar wasn't just a cat. He was a part of her soul, one of her closest friends, one who she could always depend on and now... his body grew colder by the second.

Misery consumed her and her hands crawled up to cover her head as her forehead leant on the body of Oscar, fingers tearing at the hair they became buried in. She didn't hear the Dregana land beside Xalina and Tanith and speak to them. She couldn't register the fact that they both argued against whatever had been said. She couldn't even see anything but black fur and blood.

The turmoil inside her built up until it had to come out in more than just tears. An anguished, bitter scream left her, not even slightly muffled by the direction she screamed in. A flash of pure light circled out from her body, hot enough to burn everything it hit. The heat didn't even allow time for fire to catch, it turned the plant life to charcoal instantly, Xalina, Tanith, the Dregana and the large white feline having to jump into the air to avoid being toasted. It only faded when the scream faded from her lungs and was replaced by a choked sob.

The Dregana didn't land again, instead, she merely shook her head in response to a look Xalina gave her and flew off in the direction of the Xeomont Peaks.

Tanith approached Lily cautiously before kneeling beside her and wrapping her arms around the thin frame. "I'm sorry Lil." She whispered through the tears and sniffs of the fairy.

'Sorry' did nothing for Lily.

She had been trying to help and Oscar had lost his life.

She could feel the ache of where his soul had connected to hers, like a phantom limb. Was it worth it? Looking up at her friends, Lily heard a part of her mind tell her it wasn't. What was wrong with her? How could she think that?

Trembling, she turned back to Oscar's body and gently placed it on the ground. "I need to bury him..." she finally uttered in a barely audible whisper.

"Here?"

Lily sat down on the ground and glanced around. The earth and trees were dead and scorched, hardly a pleasant place to be laid to rest. Placing her hands either side of Oscar, she pulled the corpse below ground and wound various plants into a beautiful shrine covered in colours of yellows and deep blues. Against their charred background, the colours seemed to sing to the world that there was hope and life to be cherished, something that Oscar certainly had always tried to remind Lily of.

"That's beautiful." Tanith whispered before pressing a kiss to the top of Lily's head in a way that seemed almost motherly.

Lily half smiled before letting out a long breath.

"What now?" Kiki asked.

Xalina approaches to sit on the other side of Lily with an awkward expression on her face. "The Dregana said you can't return to the mountains. She says you are too much of a danger to have around. I'm sorry Lily."

Empty silver eyes turned to look at the dark-skinned female. "Really?" An angry huff of laughter left Lily's lips. "I just risked my life to get you all out of there! I walked through that blooming grassland for so long listening to everything that was wrong with me! I've lost Oscar! And your wonderful tribe leader won't even consider helping stop a pointless war?!"

Maybe the voices were right. Maybe everything she was doing was pathetic and no one would ever be on her side. Maybe she should just give up.

No. She couldn't just give up. Oscar would have died for nothing.

Pushing herself suddenly to her feet, her face angry even as the tears glistened on her skin adding to its natural sparkle. "Fine. Whatever. I'll find another way."

"We'll come with you... You need to heal." Tanith started.

"No. Leave me alone." Lily snarled. "Go protect those who can't protect themselves. I don't need you."

Lies. She knew even in her anger she would come to regret those words. Pushing away her only human friends wasn't clever but she couldn't stop herself. Turning away from them she began to stalk off, ignoring the way they called after her, and then shedding further tears when she heard Xalina's wings beat against the ground as they took off.

"Lil..." Kiki started.

"If they aren't with me, they might not get killed because of me."

"Lil, Oscar didn't..."

"Yes, he did. He died because I took risks and I stopped paying attention!" Lily snapped. A growl shook her from the train of thought. It was considerably deeper than Kiki's and Lily realised that the great white striped beast was following them.

"What do you want?" Lily sighed, receiving no answer besides the beast walking closer and lowering itself to let her climb onto its back again. Exhaustion wasn't new to her now, but it made her body ache and her grief made her want to curl up and never wake again. The ache of her head was vicious as her emotions calmed down a little. With a nod, she clambered onto the feline and laid forwards into its fur to wrap her arms around its neck.

She didn't know where it was going to take her, but she found she really couldn't care less.

With her eyes closed, Lily couldn't tell if she was asleep or not. All she knew was the sight of the knife sliding into Oscar's body repeated like a reel, showing her the scene from different angles and all leaving her too far away to save him.

Useless. The voices whispered to her like echoes she couldn't escape. Pathetic. Failure.

She was pinned again. Bound to the spot with leather straps around her wrists. Finnigan was laughing as he held Oscar by the scruff and blood dripped from the feline. The laughter surrounded her, high and vicious.

"No!" Lily bolted upright as her dream woke her. Anger and pain blurred together overshadowing the confusion of her location.

She was in a rickety wooden shack by the looks of it, sitting on a bed that creaked with every minor movement and had sheets on it that were full of moth holes and dust.

It didn't matter though. Her mind was on something else. She had to stop Finnigan's family. The anger she felt as the images flashed through her mind again of Finnigan laughing as Oscar died pushed her out of the bed, dislodging Kiki from where she had been curled up on Lily's lap. Instantly, Lily snatched up the satchel she had kept with her and pulled out the box she kept Lucretia in.

"*Tigiri katachi*" Lily barked as the mouse fell to the ground. The moment Lucretia transformed back into her human form, Lily shot spikes of ice out of the walls, floor and ceiling until they dug into the female's skin just slightly, preventing any movement. "Try and fight back and they'll all go straight through you…"

Lucretia smirked, "Sure. You're nothing but a scared child. *Agor…*" A loud scream of pain finished her sentence as a spike shot up through her foot, slicing through flesh.

"Enough!" Lily raged. "I'm done with all of this! This war is going to end one way or another."

Lucretia snarled at the white-haired fairy, though something in her eyes changed. She could see the truth in Lily's posture. The girl who had been so timid and manipulated was not in her right mind and she was broken and desperate.

"You'll never stop it." Lucretia spat at Lily, winceing as Kiki jumped up to swipe her nose with claws in retaliation.

"Liche!" Kiki hissed, her own emotions as unstable as Lily's. "We'll stop your whole family! In the name of Oscar, I will scratch you all up if I have to."

The door to the cabin slammed open behind them and without thought, Lily moved out her hand to bind the intruder with ice as well. The intruder was nothing she expected. It was a masculine figure, standing about six and a half feet tall and glaring at her with baby blue eyes. It was human shaped with a goatee and black hair on the top of its head, however, it also had two animalistic ears, a long-striped tail, claws on its fingers and fur covering its body even though it wore shirt and trousers for dignity.

"What in wings name is that?" Kiki chimed.

"What? Well, you're very rude." The male grumbled in a deep baritone along with a roll of his eyes. "I'm who brought you here. You both passed out so I found shelter suitable for human skin. Your welcome for the burn treatment by the way."

Raising a hand to tenderly touch the burned and damaged skin where there were once long white locks, Lily narrowed her eyes, flicking them down to look at the striped tail and back up to the baby blue eyes.

"Are you…" she started, "that big cat?"

"Tiger."

"Sorry?"

The male chuckled and shook his head, "I'm a tiger, it's my species. But yes, it's a kind of 'big cat'. My name's Axel."

"Ok, I'm dreaming." Lily shook her head. Either that or the plains of insanity had really made her mad. Glancing at Lucretia, she wrapped her mouth in vines so she couldn't utter any spells and Lily turned to walk outside, releasing the strange humanoid cat and into fresh air.

Or not.

The air outside was damp, dark and close. Worst of all it was incredibly familiar. Spinning around to face Axel. "Why are we in the Densewood?!" This place almost killed her last time.

"Because no one would follow us." Axel replied calmly, folding his arms across his chest and leaning against the doorframe of the cabin. "And I'm a bigger animal than anything in here so I've been marking it as my territory."

"Eww." Kiki grimaced at the idea as she sat on Lily's shoulder. Lily, instead, shook her head.

"No. This makes no sense." Lily frowned. "How are you a half-cat? And why would you help keep us safe, you don't even know us. Are you a spy? Are you even real?"

"Wow. How long were you in the Plains of Atilavox?"

"Where?"

"The empty plains around that jail you just destroyed."

"Oh… about a month apparently?"

Axel nodded slightly with understanding dawning on his features. It unnerved Lily. Finnigan had been understanding about everything and it had been a lie.

'This one's a liar too'

It was the voice of her image echoing in her mind again. Even outside of the plains, it was loud and clear.

Sitting himself onto the ground, taking away the intimidating height he had, Axel crossed his legs and looked up at her.

"I'm real. I'm from the mainland. My race is called Vilankuri; we are animals who can turn into humans and have elemental powers." He began to explain.

"That's how you can walk in the air?" Kiki chimed.

"Yes. My magic revolves around air." Axel nodded, running his fingers through the quiffed hair on his head. "I've been locked in their place for years, and I'm banished from my home, so figured I'd help you out."

"Sure…" Lily clearly didn't believe him. She wouldn't be naive again. She wouldn't be tricked.

Her attitude caused Axel to laugh, "Can't imagine being so jaded at your age."

"You know nothing." Lily snapped.

"No. I don't." He agreed with another chuckle. "I know nothing about you other than the fact you freed an entire jail of people who had been put away for disrupting the 'natural order' of this island. And that, little ice queen, is impressive."

Lily bristled at the nickname. "I'm not an ice queen."

"Maybe. But you've made an enemy out of a lot of people and I love a good adventure and fight so I figured I'd see how this goes."

Lily and Kiki exchanged looks.

"So," Kiki tilted her head. "You helped us, because you think that us trying to stop a war might provide you with some fun?"

"Yeah."

"You're insane."

"I've been locked up with only myself for company for almost two centuries; your stint in the plains have nothing on me," Axel grinned in a way that was both unhinged and playful.

"And this is supposed to make us trust you?"

Axel shrugged. "Trust me, don't trust me. I don't really care. But I am the only reason there's no dark-dwelling predators surrounding this place right now."

Lily glanced around the Densewood. As expected, she couldn't see far, but she could appreciate that she didn't feel like she was being watched by something just out of reach.

"Fine." Lily huffed, "Be a guard cat if it makes you happy. Just don't get in my way." Pushing passed the male and back inside where Lucretia glared at her instantly.

"Tell me where these people are." Lily held up the scroll with all the family names on it. Pulling the vine away so Lucretia could speak, Lily snarled as she received a face full of spit once more.

"Fine, stay in here and freeze." Lily grumbled with a roll of her eyes, before turning to leave the cabin.

She didn't like this.

There was no escape.

Lucretia was inside. Axel outside. And viparterkas lingered out of what Axel was currently claiming to be 'his territory'. Ignoring the man, Lily took herself up into the treeline with Kiki and settled down in the canopy, her legs pulled close leaving just enough space for Kiki to curl up between them and Lily's torso.

"I can't believe he's gone." Kiki whispered tearfully.

"I keep hoping I'll wake up to find all this a bad dream. But, it's so hollow in my chest. It feels like part of me has been cut out."

"I know."

"You feel it too?"

Kiki hummed her confirmation before curling up tighter into a ball as Lily folded herself over to rest her forehead on her knees and allow more tears to spill.

If Lily had thought she had cried a lot during her time in the plains, it was nothing compared to the tears which fell every time she was out of sight of anyone but Kiki over the next few weeks. Each day, trying to convince Lucretia to tell her where her relatives lived failed, the woman even taking to spitting food back in Lily's face.

Frustration settled into her core alongside the desperation and hopelessness rippling from the empty part of her soul. The only part of her that did any healing was the burn. The skin knitted together nicely with the strange medicine Axel created from plants unknown to Lily, but her hair made no sign of growing there again. She may have that panel of hair missing for the rest of her life; though the symbolism and irony wasn't lost on her. She'd lost a part of her soul with Oscar's last breath, it might as well show on her physically.

Axel didn't speak much, in fact, he spent most of his time in the tiger form she had met him in. He was easier to be around in that form. Lily trusted the animal in him much more than the human.

"You could just get rid of her and go searching for the others." Axel brought it up one night after he had brought back a hunt and cooked it over a fire so Lily would be able to digest it.

"No. I've never killed anyone and I don't plan to start now… and if I did, I wouldn't start with her." She added in an undertone, the face of the man who haunted her nightmares flashing in front of her eyes. No, she'd start with Finnigan. The very thought of him these days burned hot with rage mixed in with the numb feeling of grief for Oscar.

"Whoever's made such an innocent face able to look that venomous really has it coming, huh?" Axel whistled lightly as he laid back on the ground, tearing off meat from the bone of his prey. "What did they do?"

"That's not your business." Lily grumbled, folding her arms across her chest defensively.

"Ok, got it." Axel shrugged with a sigh. He never asked too much which honestly made him tolerable to have around. He never followed when Lily walked off to find a quiet space to cry, and he had never come within five feet of her in his humanoid form.

"You could use that mind control spell?"

Lily looked at Kiki who had finished her portion of meat and was looking at the cabin with her head tilted to the side in thought.

"That only controls physical actions," Lily shook her head.

"There's a spell to force someone to tell the truth to any question." Axel piped up.

"Really?"

"They used it on me when they first caught me, kept using it until I passed out and took tiger form, then I refused to change back so they muzzled me and left me there." Axel growled, his admission filling Lily with a softer emotion than anything she had felt in weeks.

"I'm sorry. No one deserves that." She whispered.

"Oh, not such an ice queen?"

"Shut up."

Axel barked a laugh before sobering and getting back on topic. "'*Fitipra*' was the incantation they used on me then."

"If I use that spell I would completely take away her free will." Lily pointed out.

"Having her sit there in the dark until she gives in is just breaking her will." Axel countered. "Better to take it for a second and have her hate you for it after?"

Lily mused over the reality of that statement for a few seconds in silence. "We can't let her go after though, can we?"

"No." Kiki chimed. "We can't. And we'll have to stop any in the locations she gives us."

"How do we stop so many people?"

"Keep turning them into mice for now, I suppose."

"Then what? Keep them?"

"At least they can't kill anyone else as mice. And if they escape, I can catch them." Kiki chortled at the idea though quickly looked guilty at Lily's defeated words.

"So, they'll be our prisoners…"

"We'll come up with something better I'm sure."

"You think? Everything keeps getting worse, I don't see how this wouldn't do the same."

"You want to stop a war, you can't be as nice as you want to be." Axel interrupted sternly.

Lily dropped her head into her hands, arms supported by her elbows against her thighs. "I know. I just… I don't like it." Kiki nuzzled into Lily for a while, providing her comfort and companionship. Finally, Lily sighed in defeat. "Ok. The truth spell it is."

Stepping back into the cabin felt like stepping up to execution. Lily knew that the moment she did this, she would cross a line she could never come back from. To take someone's free will from them completely, to control them outright... even she hadn't felt that level of control loss when she had been bound by Finnigan. Despite the pain, the terror, the weakness, she had still been able to have her own mind.

"I'm so sorry." She whispered as the vine pulled away from Lucretia's mouth and Lily pressed her fingertips to the woman's forehead.

"Fitipra"

Having control of someone was strange. It felt like a war within your own mind, like your brain was being pulled in all sorts of directions and it was difficult to stay in control. It was painful, and there was a sickly part of Lily that knew it was exhilarating. Mostly though, it was loud. The screams of a mind trying to fight her out were almost as loud as the echoing voices from the plains. They brought tears to Lily's eyes as she persisted. She didn't want to. She didn't like it. But she'd committed to stopping this war, Oscar was dead because of it, she couldn't turn back now.

Tell me where the Byrnes are!

Lucretia resisted, Lily's eyes boring into hers, then she parted her lips and gave five location names. "Quintegia, Mythanissiam, The Fae Greenwood, Fangawa and Kita-Utara". The horror and anger on her face was unmissable, but Lily withdrew, having gotten her information.

"Tikusoma Svica". The moment Lucretia transformed into a mouse again, Kiki pounced on her and put her back in the container, slamming it shut with her paw.

"So, we have places to start..." Kiki sighed.

Placing Lucretia's cage back in the satchel, Lily swung it over her shoulder, "Yeah. Let's go." Lily's eyes were dull, as though a part of the spark of her life had gone. Was that new? Or had that happened when Oscar died? Kiki sighed softly and followed her out of the cabin.

Chapter 11: Kita-Utara

"Where are we going first?" Kiki queried after a long stretch of heavy silence. Axel had shifted forms and walked below Lily on the ground keeping an ear out for threats.

"Kita-Utara. It's the closest town to the mountains, therefore the closest to us."

"And how do we find the Byrnes?"

"Well, we know disguises work... I doubt they'll expect to find me in a larger town." Lily half chortled, her fingers dancing over the healing skin on the side of her head. It was still reddened and scabbed, but the paste Axel had made her was doing wonders for the pain and the speed of healing. Apparently, as his kind could only control one element, they had developed many medicines that required zero magic involvement. Lily's mind went back to the man with his ill wife, perhaps the medicine he wanted the flowers for was created in a similar way.

Lily also found herself wondering if his wife had gotten better. Losing a soulmate wasn't something she would wish on anyone... not even Finnigan and she was confident that he was the reason she'd lost one of her soulmates.

"Oh no... what are you going to turn me into?" Kiki gulped, pulling Lily out of her thoughts.

"Well, I can remember the words for snake and raven now... so you'll be one and Axel will be the other."

"I don't need to be an animal." Axel chimed from beneath them in his humanoid form.

"You'll stand out like that more than you would as a tiger." Lily rolled her eyes.

"I can become fully human," He informed her indignantly.

Lily jumped down from the branches to stand in front of him with an eyebrow raised. "You what?"

"I have a fully human form."

"So why do you walk around like that?"

"I prefer it." Axel commented bluntly, raising an eyebrow in return as though daring Lily to judge his choice. Instead, she let out a small laugh.

"Fair enough." She shrugged. "A human form will help us out a lot. As far as anyone is concerned, Lily 'the traitor' travels alone. So, if I'm disguised and walking around with you it'll mask suspicions even more." Folding her arms across her chest, Lily nodded at the male. "Come on then, let's see this human form."

"You're very demanding…" Axel laughed.

"I have very little time and patience left." Lily deadpanned, though she was relieved that Axel didn't seem annoyed at her quickly-diminishing positivity.

"Yeah yeah, stop the war. I know." Axel rolled his eyes before closing them and focusing on changing his body. Fur receded along with the ears, tail and claws, leaving a tall and incredibly handsome man. He still had the goatee against softly tanned skin and his muscular body showed itself to a high degree without the fur masking it from sight.

"You'll still stand out..." Lily commented with a shake of her head.

"Oh?"

"You look too good. Like, magical good even in a magical world."

"Why, thank you."

"I'm not complimenting you."

"It sounds like you are." Axel teased despite the irritated glare he gained from the girl.

"I'm saying you will get people's attention and we don't need that." Lily chided.

"Ok, so you get me a hooded cloak and I let my beard grow scraggy until I look like a homeless punk?" Axel smiled down at her, his grin just as cheeky as it was when he was covered in fur.

"Cloak would make you suspicious... ragged clothes and an unkept beard might help."

"Rags? Really?" Axel whined.

"You can always leave."

Axel frowned before sighing in defeat. "Damn. You're such a grump. Thankfully, that doesn't put me off in the slightest and I still think this is more fun than anything I'd be doing while wandering the world alone."

"Glad to be of assistance..." Lily deadpanned before handing over the coat she had been carrying since the mountains. Axel took hold of it and was clearly going to comment about how her small size wouldn't fit him, but he didn't get the words out before Lily had tapped the coat with the end of her scythe and muttered *'Textilce'* redesigning the garment into something thinner but larger so Axel could wear it on his torso. He curled his lip slightly at the brown and tan coloured tunic he was holding before giving in without protest and shrugging it onto his body.

"You can show off to women after the war has been stopped." Lily grumbled.

"Who said it's women I'd show off to?"

Axel laughed loudly at the look of surprise that moved over Lily's face followed by a look of understanding guilt.

"Sorry." Lily mumbled. "Shouldn't assume."

Ruffling her hair and receiving a smack to his hand, Axel grinned again, adjusting his tunic as he began walking. "All good. I happen to like both."

"I don't know what I like..."

"You literally just looked through me like my body didn't exist. I reckon you like personality and connections rather than the body."

Lily glanced up at the man with a confused expression on her face.

"Some people feel connections to the soul rather than any attraction to the physical body of another person." Axel explained though he merely got a curious musing expression from Lily before she looked away. Was that what she felt? It certainly had been the lie of a personality of Finnigan that had drawn her in, though she couldn't deny she had found his green eyes intoxicatingly beautiful.

"There's so much about this world I don't know." She whispered softly, almost sadly.

"You seem to know more than most on this island." Axel reassured, though the air around Lily was heavy. Something Kiki took care of when she fluttered down to match their heights and huffed.

"I've decided, if you make me a snake, I will bite everyone I see. I want legs at least!"

Lily snorted with the sudden laughter in her throat as she looked at the indigent cat who had obviously missed the rest of the conversation. "Ok. Raven it is. You still won't be able to talk though."

"Yeah, but that will also help the disguise. It won't be possible for anyone to hear me talk back to you." Kiki sighed dramatically. "Though how you will cope without hearing my voice for a while I cannot imagine."

"It will be the hardest thing I'll ever endure," Lily teased.

"It better be, or I will peck you."

"Well, now that's just mean." Lily laughed, reaching out to nudge the feline gently with her hand. Even as a raven Kiki would be good to have around.

It took a week to walk to Kita-Utara, and once they had come into open plains, Lily had disguised them as intended. Her hair was black, the burn on the side of her head masked as a chosen style, her eyes blue to match Axel's, her shimmer hidden behind slightly tanned skin. Axel had kept his promise and let his beard grow over the days, it wasn't long and unkempt yet, but it certainly was starting to hide some of his facial features. Lily smirked now and then at the odd grey hair that grew in it, asking just how old Axel actually was.

Turned out he was over three hundred years old, his kind living for near eight-hundred in general.

Axel had been in the jail long enough to have heard the stories from two of the century wars of the island, and long enough that he'd spent two-thirds of his life there.

Lily could understand why he was aiming to just enjoy life. After so long of nothing, surely anyone would want to have fun where they could.

Her attitude softened a little at the information; he had suffered more than anyone she knew by being left there alone for so long. It was any wonder he wasn't more unstable. Lily wasn't sure she would have survived with her sanity. Heck, she wasn't sure she had survived the Plains of Atilavox or Oscar's death with her sanity. Her thoughts jumped all over the place, they were irrational and the voices still spoke to her. Even now they told her that her plan was going to fail because she was useless and nothing but a burden.

"So how we playing this? Travelling siblings?" Axel hissed as they approached the great wooden gates of Kita-Utara. The settlement seemed older, designed more of wood than stone, possibly due to stone holding the cold of the environment.

"Fleeing villages overrun by the military?"

"Good reasoning. I'll be the protective older brother, you can be the bratty little sister."

"Excuse me?"

"Well you have an attitude, so it'll fit."

Lily rolled her eyes at the comment. It wasn't that she had an attitude, she just hadn't had the mental and emotional energy to try and make Axel like her. She had so much on her mind that thoughts of pleasing people weren't at the forefront for the first time in her life.

Letting the black hair fall over her face a little, left scruffy and back combed to hide her ears even with the missing panel of hair, Lily stuffed her hands into the black trousers she had created and slouched her shoulders.

"See, grumpy sister indeed." Axel chortled, slinging his arm around her like a playful brother might and pulled her through the gates and into the outskirts of the town. "Besides, the less attention you get, the better. It's bad enough that we've got to excuse your 'companion' being in a cage. At least if you aren't nice, I can claim the snake isn't either."

Lily glanced down at the satchel where Lucretia remained. They had turned her into a snake so that there were two 'companion animals' for two 'witches' and Lily had fashioned two false wands for them to carry but hopefully not need to use. Kiki ruffled her feathers in light protest, not liking that she was having to pretend to be Axel's companion in the plan. But still, she perched on his shoulder without much discomfort.

"With you as a brother, it's no wonder I have an attitude." Lily grumbled, ignoring the snort of amusement from Axel as he dragged them to a building which looked much like a tavern.

Inside, both of them froze in their step at the sight of the person behind the bar and the man sitting to the side.

"You're not witches!" Lily exclaimed as she approached.

The bartender was six foot in height, with long forest-green hair and pointed ears that reached upwards from her head, unhidden at all by the hair like Lily's were. She also had fangs that flashed into sight as she spoke to the male companion. He shared her length of ears, with his long purple hair pulled back into a ponytail, making no effort to hide the features. His purple eyes glinted with amusement as they turned to look at the little fairy. Though it was the green-haired beauty who spoke.

"If you can see that, then neither are you." Her voice was deep for a typical female, and her smirk was surprisingly mischievous as she examined them both.

"But… this is a witch town!" Lily hissed, looking around at the customers in the tavern. There were not many due to the time of day, but they were witches.

"That's what everyone is meant to think." The bartender chuckled, before pulling out a couple of glasses to set on the counter. "What can I get you?"

"Oh, mead please!" Axel chimed.

"What? No. Wait." Lily stammered as she looked at Axel like he was insane for just taking this in their stride.

"Have a drink, then we'll have a chat." The purple-haired male spoke, his face tired but his voice stern. Lily swallowed under his scrutiny before looking at the lime-green eyes of the bartender.

"Just water... thanks."

"Exotic." The bartender rolled her eyes with a chuckle before pouring out the two requested drinks. Once she handed them over, she motioned for them to follow her behind the bar and into the back room. The purple-haired male stood to flank them from behind, showing his insane height of what must have been close to seven feet. Lily officially felt like a child as she walked with them, but it only made her stand straighter as though that would help her.

The back room was cramped, hardly enough space to fit the four of them, filled with shelves of various bottles and flasks. The bartender jumped up to sit on the side next to a safe where she likely kept the takings of the tavern. The purple-haired male leant against the doorway, both to keep an eye on the tavern and it almost felt he was specifically blocking Axel, Lily and Kiki in.

It felt like if they said the wrong answers, they wouldn't leave this room. Lily shuddered at the thought as it crossed her mind.

"So, you two look like witches. But you can see us. What are you?" The bartender spoke with a slight amused curl of her lip which showed off the fang on the right side.

"Vilankuri." Axel answered, really taking all this in his stride.

Lily glanced from him, to the raven on his shoulder and back to the green haired being. She didn't really have much choice, did she?

"Fairy," she answered, not missing the raised eyebrow she received. "I was born without wings." She explained the unspoken question.

"Ah. So, you're the terrible traitor everyone's talking about?"

Lily chewed on her lower lip, though she didn't need to answer that obvious question before the bartender continued.

"From the rumours, anyone would think you were eight foot and dressed like death itself. True you have a scythe?"

Lily let out a small laugh at the description. Were the rumours that bad already? Pulling out her 'wand' she muttered the spell to turn it back to its original form, displaying the charred scythe for them to see. The green-haired being let out a low whistle of approval before chortling to herself.

"Touché. Well, I'm Liserli. I'm an ancient who's a mixed race of people you'd never have heard of. And Pyran here is the same, but he was born to someone under the influence of the Morequacor so have certain mind abilities." She explained. "He has control over this whole town enough to mask anyone who isn't a witch against the witches. It's a bit of a safe haven for wayward souls, but also stays completely under the radar of any discrimination."

"The Morequacor isn't real," Lily interrupted.

"Oh, it is." Pyran spoke up. "It's just not what the legends think it is and it has powers you wouldn't guess. I only heard about it from my mother and I still doubt I understand it."

Lily raised an eyebrow at him. If it was real, had she really seen it back then on the beach? But if it wasn't what the legends said, why would it show itself to a girl who felt like she was about to die?

Liserli's eyes narrowed a little as she coughed to get the attention back on her. "You're welcome to stay. The rules are simple. You do not give anyone away for what they really are. If you mess up, I will slaughter you myself." Her fangs flashed in warning as she smiled at them.

Lily gulped. That wasn't a threat. That was a promise.

"I don't want to out anyone. I'm looking for a specific family." Whether it was because they weren't witches, or whether it was because they were obviously aware of the way those who were different were treated, Lily wasn't sure, but something made her spill her story to Liserli and Pyran. Perhaps she truly was desperately grabbing at any string that might provide her with some support in her endeavour. Part way through, Pyran vacated the room to go and take orders from anyone who had approached the bar, but Liserli listened with a seemingly bored expression.

"So that's the reason the war keeps happening. I did think the insistence of racism was odd from the officials."

"Racism?"

"The discrimination of other humanoid races and cultures due to differences, basically." Liserli shrugged. "All the officials here are so against anyone who isn't a witch it's intense. It's only gotten worse since you came on the scene."

Lily winced at the guilt that shot through her. "Are any of the officials called Byrne?"

Liserli mused the question for a moment before shaking her head. "Doesn't ring a bell."

"I was told some resided here." Lily cursed, pulling out the family tree from her satchel and spread it out to the side of Liserli. "What about any of these names?"

"And what, exactly, do I get out of this little exchange?"

Lily blinked up at the lime green eyes. Silence in the little room was only broken by the angry flapping of Kiki's wings.

"What?"

"This war doesn't affect me. I just take a holiday and then come back and build another tavern under a different disguise." Liserli leaned back against the shelves and folded her arms across her chest. "So, what do I get for sticking my neck out and helping you find an ancient, well connected and powerful family? I have no interest in being on their radar."

"But people will die!"

"People die every day." Liserli countered. "I don't see anyone risking their neck to change those."

"Lily probably would if she had an idea how…" Axel chuckled.

"Idealistic idiocracy." Liserli dismissed, pushing herself off the side and heading back for the tavern's main room. "Well good luck to you. Feel free to pay for a room while you stay."

Lily stared at the doorway incredulously. Her brain seemed to be stuck in place like a record that had been damaged.

'Useless.'

'Just give up.'

'No one cares.'

"How can she not care?!" Lily demanded aloud, drowning out the voices in her mind and turning to look at Axel as though expecting him to have an answer for her. Though she quickly snorted and shook her head, "Why am I asking you? You don't care either, you're just here for fun."

Rolling up the scroll and stuffing it back into her satchel, Lily stormed out of the little back room and out of the tavern without looking back. She just about registered the flutter of wings before Kiki perched onto her shoulder to ride wherever Lily was headed.

Every single person she seemed to meet cared more about themselves than the unnecessary slaughter of thousands of fairies and witches. Their lifestyle or their beliefs or whatever were never worth risking. How selfish could the world get?!

'You're one to talk. What if you are wrong and your actions are selfishly going to get people around you killed?'

She hated that the main little voice in her head belonged to Finnigan Byrne. No matter the months that went by, she couldn't get him to stop haunting her. Every time she heard his voice in her mind, her neck constricted at the memory of being bound.

"I'm not wrong." She growled under her breath at nothing while turning down a dark alley where it would be quiet and out of the main public eye. Sitting down on the ground, Lily cast her eyes up to watch the clouds rolling in with the promise of rain. Kiki fluttered down to perch on her knee and watch her with her head tilted to the side. Lily had been teasing, but right now she wished she could transform Kiki back so they could talk.

"Am I doing this all wrong?" She asked the raven who cawed back in response. Should she conform and do what was best for herself in spite of the world? What was better for her would be to leave and never come back. She wished she had decided to leave back on the Xeomont peaks. If she had, Oscar would still be there.

Leaning forward to press her nose against the raven's beak and the only thing left in her vision was the face of her soul companion, Lily sighed.

"You just need to be more realistic." The deep voice made her jump, putting her on edge as Axel sat down beside her. "You are much more likely to get people on board if they can see a benefit for themselves or their loved ones. If the risk outweighs the benefits then they won't want to risk it."

"It's wrong."

"Maybe. But that's how people survive." Axel shrugged, his eyes suggesting he knew this more intimately than he was giving away.

Droplets of rain began to hit their faces as silence engulfed.

"Liserli's agreed to help." Axel half whispered.

"What? How?" Lily started.

"I threatened her." Axel stated bluntly. "I made the benefit outweigh the risk."

Lily blinked up at him in surprise. "But... that's..."

"Wrong?" Axel supplied with a chuckle. "What's right and wrong is a very grey area, and in this case, surely the greater good of getting the Byrnes outweighs the threats?"

Lily chewed her lip. That was how she had justified forcing Lucretia to tell her where her relations could be found, but it still didn't sit right with her. She didn't like that she was having to become someone who could cause such negativities for others. She wanted to take those away from people. She didn't want them to feel threats like she had in her life, she didn't want them to be as out of control as she had been, she didn't want to use and abuse like Finnigan had used and abused her.

"What did you threaten her with?" Lily whispered.

"Exposure. I told her how long they'll keep her locked up and it seems she rather enjoys her freedom." Axel shrugged.

"If you exposed her, you'd expose everyone else using this as a haven."

"Yup."

Lily groaned at the concept; so many innocents would be affected by that threat if he carried it out.

"Stop complaining. It got us what we need." Axel scolded.

"At this rate, we'll be the villains."

"Lily. Check reality; you are already the villain in everyone's eyes. You're the danger and the threat that everyone is hunting and/or scared of. You heard her, the rumours make you sound like 'death itself'" Axel stared her down, serious in expression and more logical than Lily was letting herself be. "Plus, your plan is to invade settlements, kidnap members of an ancient family and cage them in mouse form until you can force them to give up their life-expanding plots. You better start accepting that you aren't a 'good little girl' anymore and the world isn't all sunshine and rainbows."

"I'm aware of that." Lily growled.

"Being aware of it and accepting it are two different things."

"Well, maybe I don't want to accept it."

"Then you'll be butting heads with the world for the rest of your life. Or it'll destroy you."

"You're really not helping my mood." Lily huffed, leaning her head against Kiki's feathered body.

"Wasn't really trying to." Axel laughed. Pushing himself to his feet, he offered a hand out to Lily. "So, we doing this?"

With a sigh, Lily took the hand offered and pulled herself to her feet.

"Can't justify turning back now." She concluded, the weight of Oscar's lost presence pushing her forward.

With an encouraging nod, Axel led her back to the tavern she had stormed out of. Pyran had moved away from the bar and settled himself in the far corner, his feet up on the table and a steaming mug of drink just within reach.

Liserli raised an unimpressed eyebrow as the two approached the bar. "Show me the names then." She grumbled, clearly not happy about the fact Axel had managed to threaten her. How exactly he had managed it, Lily couldn't quite imagine, Liserli looked like she would rather rip out your jugular than be threatened. But the wary gaze she gave Axel suggested he had actually found power over her.

"Thank you." Lily mumbled awkwardly, pulling out the scroll and spreading it out on the bar for Liserli to peruse.

A mere hum was all the response she received while Liserli pulled the scroll closer and let her lime eyes run over the names on there.

"I take it the ones crossed out in blood red aren't around anymore?" She asked with a mildly accusing tone.

"No. It seems if any of them go against the war, Quintina or Cyrus wipe them off the family tree." Lily explained.

"Oh? They kill their own kids?" Liserli seemed genuinely surprised.

"What? You think I did it?" Lily challenged. "I'm seventeen. How could I have gotten to that many people even if I was a killer?"

Liserli surveyed Lily's irritated expression for a moment before finally chuckling. "You've got an attitude, kid. I kinda like you."

"I'm not sure that's a compliment…" Lily grumbled, making both Axel and Liserli laugh aloud. These weren't the kinds of people she thought she would be allied with, but she'd have to take what she could.

"Well, hate to say it but I'm not sure of any of these names," Liserli turned the scroll back to Lily. "However, I've had different names over the years to fool people into thinking I'm not that old; so, I would check out the family in the biggest house in town. They have family members on the town's council and they own a lot of the property here as well. I think one of the sons is high in the military as well."

Reaching over she placed the tip of her finger against one of the names on the page: 'Alexander'. "One of them is nicknamed 'Lexi' though it doesn't match with the name he claims as his birth name. Could possibly be this guy?"

Lily nodded as she examined the name in question. It hadn't occurred to her that the older members of the Byrne family would be using other names to hide their true identity but now Liserli pointed it out it made complete sense.

"That's somewhere to start, but how am I going to check a whole family?" Lily mused.

"They're always hiring maids." Liserli smirked. "Apparently, the grandmother is very hard to work for and she chases most maids out without a few weeks. Perfect cover for going in and investigating and then leaving so soon?"

"A maid?"

"Yup. She makes them do all the work without magic too, so it won't be fun."

"None of this has been fun…" Lily commented dryly.

"Well then!" Liserli smirked. "The oldest sister drinks here, I'll mention that I have a new lodger who's looking for some work. Though, you may want to cover that short side of your hair. The magic here works to hide your pointed ears, luckily for you, but anything out of the norm will get you more attention than you want."

Lily touched the burned side of her head before nodding. She could arrange her hair in a centre parting to cover it.

"And you'll need a different name, obviously." Liserli handed over a key to one of the inn rooms and left Lily and Axel at the end of the bar to go and talk to someone else who approached. Lily stared down at the key. Just one? Again. She was expected to stay in the same room as someone else? At least this one wasn't lying to her face and charming her heart out of her chest.

And he could sleep in tiger form.

"You're relegating me to the floor, aren't you?" Axel frowned as though reading her mind.

With a playful, sarcastic grin, Lily turned to him and closed her hand around the key. "I wouldn't be a bratty sister if I didn't." Taking hold of the scroll, Lily headed up the stairs to the far side of the room to search for the room, leaving Axel to finish his mead on his own.

Chapter 12: Flames of Trauma

It turned out that being a maid for this family was so much worse that Lily had imagined. She had been introduced to them as Emira Hawkes, but she had yet to be called by either the first or surname. Instead she was referred to as 'maid' or 'you'.

Not only were the family rude, the rules they set in place were borderline ridiculous at times.

Companion animals were to stay in the maid's quarters at all times. Lily was not allowed to have her wand on her outside of her room. She had to complete all tasks manually. She couldn't look any family member in the eye without receiving a stern swat from the grandmother's cane. She had to eat in her quarters and only once her duties were done for the period of the day. The same applied to drinks and bathroom needs.

Despite the fact the house had three floors and too many rooms to be necessary, Lily realised quickly that she was the only maid and so the workload was extortionate.

No wonder everyone left.

But there were so many travellers who passed through town that the family could always find someone desperate enough for money to last between one and three months. Perhaps if there weren't so many passers-by to use, the family would have to rethink their management style. Of course, if that was the case, Lily wouldn't be able to have a pretty valid excuse to leave from day one if she found the information out quickly.

Nothing happened that quickly. That would make Lily far luckier than she was.

"Still nothing?" Axel asked on one of the rare visits Lily was allowed. Lily couldn't leave the estate, but her family was permitted to visit for an hour every other day so long as it didn't interfere with how much work she got done.

"No. I've cleaned this place top to bottom and I've found nothing to say they might be Byrne's... other than their attitudes." Lily added bitterly as she poured tea into a cup for herself and settled into the uncomfortable chair given to her quarters.

"Maybe they've got a hidden room." Axel supplied.

"I've kept an eye out while cleaning and Kiki has been browsing at night when she can be changed back to a cat." Lily sighed. "I've found some... enlightening stuff... but nothing that actually helps me." Axel laughed at the shudder that ran through her at the memory of some of the objects and attire she had found while cleaning and washing. The whole family, frankly, had no shame even around a stranger like her. If she commented, she faced consequences.

"'Enlightening' sounds fun." Axel chortled.

"Maybe for some people; doesn't appeal to me." Lily stuck her tongue out a little in disgust at the ideas of some things she'd seen.

"You're so dull."

"Whatever."

Axel shook his head and took a sip of the tea he had been given. It was obvious that he would prefer something with a stronger taste. "What about a basement or attic?"

"Can't find an entrance to either; which makes me think that's exactly what I should be looking for." Lily admitted.

"You'll have to start following the family and see if they lead you somewhere new."

That seemed like a good, logical suggestion. But a couple of weeks later when Lily found herself pinned to the wall of a basement stairway, she regretted ever listening to the tiger.

She had changed up her routines to make the chores follow the members of the family around the house. Never so she was in the way, but so she could hear if they ventured into a room she wasn't aware of yet. Lily messed up though.

She messed up badly.

The smirk on Lexi's face told her just how badly.

"You know, there's easier ways to get my attention than stalking me." He purred with eyes the same green as the ones that haunted her memory.

"I wasn't…" she squirmed, pushing herself further against the wall in an attempt to put space between them.

"You don't have to lie." He raised his hand and brushed his fingers over her cheek, stepping forward to trap her body with his own. "You're one of the prettier maids we've had, so I don't mind."

"No." Lily pulled his hand away from her face with her eyes turning to a light glare. The trapped feeling was turning her stomach and the glint in his eyes was ominous at best. She had to get out of here.

Lexi laughed darkly. "You want to still deny it? Are we playing that kind of game?"

Game? What game?! How in any sense was this a game?! As he leant down to catch her lips with his, Lily shoved his chest, the spell to reject/eject a target screaming in her mind and sending Lexi crashing into the wall behind him.

"Don't touch me!" Lily snarled. Though instantly her throat was closed by long fingers wrapping around them as Lexi launched himself back towards her, his strength lifting her a little from the ground.

"You liche! How dare you?" Lexi snarled at her. But it was no longer Lexi who Lily saw. Despite his blond hair that fell in his face and the stubble that framed his face, she saw brown hair and soft skin. She saw Finnigan. Those green hues full of hate, and the pressure around her neck that merged memory with reality.

He was going to kill her this time.

Her hands flew up to claw at the hold around her throat. His lips were moving but the sound was drowned by the ringing in her ears.

Finnigan had already killed part of her. He was going to finish the job.

The feeling of a hand on her thigh was enough to trigger the transition from being stuck in her mind to reacting. She had to escape. He couldn't bind her again. He couldn't take anything else from her. Pulling against the one finger pressing most onto her voice box, she managed to utter the *Agora* spell. A yell of pain echoed in the stairwell followed by the sudden release of her neck. Her legs didn't catch her. With thuds of bone against wood, Lily clattered down the stairs to the basement as the scent of burning buried her.

She had to keep him away.

He couldn't take more from her.

Her hands dug into her hair as she curled up into a ball on the cold floor. She could hear the crackling of fire above her, she could tell it was spreading through the house, but she couldn't stop.

Finnigan couldn't be allowed to touch her again.

The fire sprung forth and devoured anything in its wake. It was something that could keep the threat far away from her, even if the roof above began to crumble. The idea of being buried alive didn't scare Lily as much as those green eyes did.

Besides, maybe it would be best to die now. She couldn't lose anything else that way.

"Em!"

"Emira!"

Why was someone calling that name?

Why would someone even bother coming for her?

She'd walked away from anyone who had ever cared about her or she had cared for. With smoke-filled lungs, she couldn't call back, she could only allow sleep to take her.

"Lily!"

~

Axel had actually been enjoying Kita-Utara. He worked in the bar and got on well with Liserli despite the threats he had made towards her. For the most part, the locals were pleasant and he discovered that there really were more races of people hidden in plain sight. He had played cards with a draconian and a married couple from the mainland, though they wouldn't tell him what they were. He had spotted a couple of fairies and even another of his own kind. A snow leopard with a playful attitude.

"You going to leave when you've saved up enough?" The snow leopard, known as Quinn, asked one night over a drink. The story Axel told everyone was that he and his sister had only stopped travelling because they needed funds but they were still intending on continuing to Mythanissiam to find relatives. Of course, any non-witch knew that wasn't the full truth, but they all believed they were just here for funds. Liserli hadn't sold out who Lily was.

"This place is pretty cool." Axel admitted. "I don't think Emira feels particularly safe in one place for too long though."

Thinking of the little he knew of her, Lily didn't seem like she really knew what it was like to be safe and accepted no matter where she had been. She was hurt deeply, Axel could smell it on her even as she walked ahead of him as though confident in her direction. He heard her whimpers at night when she spoke the same name over again, a name she never once uttered when she was awake.

'Finn'.

Whomever 'Finn' was, he had done a lot of damage to the teen. On top of that she'd been banished from her home, lost friends and even lost part of her soul.

"I wouldn't be able to sit still after that." Axel mumbled, receiving a confused look from the white-haired man.

"Is that why you are sticking with her?" Quinn asked. Most felines like themselves didn't attach to others. Feline Vilankuri were often solitary creatures who came together for mating only. Quinn, himself, lived on the outskirts of the town and was often seen enjoying his alone time.

"Nah." Axel chuckled. "She's fun to wind up and she sees lots of places."

Quinn raised an eyebrow in disbelief.

"Tch. Ok, so I also think she could use having someone at her back. We aren't close enough that she's scared of the effects on me." Axel admitted with a roll of his eyes. "Oh, you could come with?"

"Huh? Why?"

Axel shrugged.

"Maybe if you told me what you were really doing, I might. But you..." Before he could finish, the sound of yelling rushed in from outside. It sounded panicked and, when they looked outside, they could see people running in the same direction.

"What the...?" Both men were on their feet and in the tavern doorway in an instant. Both could smell the problem as soon as the door opened.

Smoke filled the air.

The smell of burning made Axel choke the moment it hit the back of his throat.

"It's coming from the mansion!"

"Water magic isn't working!"

The mansion…

"Damn!" Axel jumped out of the doorway and began to sprint towards the place he had visited Lily many times already. He could feel his blood pounding through his veins as he got a horrible sinking feeling. Lily had to be alright… right?

"You go cover downstairs, I'll go up!" Quinn yelled over the crackling as he caught up to Axel who had slowed with his eyes wide and reflecting the flames that licked the air and drowned out the sounds of anyone inside.

"Right!" Axel agreed, pushing his legs into motion.

She'd be fine. They would find her before it was too late.

Why was the idea of losing her scary? He hadn't even cared about whether someone stuck around. But the idea of her losing her life in the fire filled him with sickening dread.

She was so young. Naive? Yes. Idealistic? Completely. But she was also so incredibly brave. Facing tough decisions even though they killed her and still having the strength to take another step for the good of others… From Axel's experience, that didn't exist in many people.

"Emira!" He called through downstairs, manipulating the air around him to keep the smoke away from his lungs and the fire away from his skin.

The whole place reeked of smoke and barbeque. The fact that the main family hadn't made it out said to Axel that there was no way Lily had.

Blasting air through doorways to rip burning wood from its joints, he searched the living quarters, the kitchen, the laundrette, the dining rooms, the reading rooms…

"There's too many rooms!" He cursed, turning on his heels as he reached a side door to the gardens. Should he check the gardens? Hopping to the side as the floor crumbled under his foot. Nope. This building wasn't going to last. He had to find her.

"Axel!" The shout from Quinn was muffled in the crackling of the fire, but it was enough for the tiger to run through the house and up to the next floor.

"Which way?!" He called back, unable to smell anything other than smoke, burning material and meat.

"Down here!"

The voice came from the left. It didn't take long before Axel skidded to a halt beside Quinn who was pointing at a burning tapestry where a blonde man lay motionless beneath.

"I'll get you through." Quinn called over the noise, holding out his hand and creating a gust of ice wind to smother and freeze the tapestry. "My ice magic won't last long in this heat though."

"Got it. Thanks." Axel nodded before pushing through the tapestry, feeling the burn of both ice and fire as he shifted from one to the other. The stairs behind had been eaten away by fire. Great. Jumping with a leap of faith into the darkness, Axel was glad to discover that it wasn't that deep.

"Lily!" He called instinctively as he spotted the outline of her body on the hot stone.

Her body was still, her breath shallow.

"Lily!"

He cursed, hoisting her up over his shoulder before heading back to the entrance.

"Quinn! Grab her!" He called up, waiting for the lithe, tall body of his friend to appear. Quinn laid himself down on the ground and froze his legs to the ground so he could lean his entire top half of his body over the edge and reach down. Between two men over six feet, Axel was able to pass Lily up. "Get her out!"

With a nod, Quinn pulled Lily up out of the strange room filled with smoke. No fire though. Stamping his foot on the ground, Axel sent a blast of air through the room, pushing the smoke out of the entrance and leaving him in a surprisingly intact room.

"Lily must have set the fire and directed it away from her." Which meant she couldn't have been unconscious for long.

"She did."

Axel jumped at the voice and spun around to squint into the darkness of the room. His eyes weren't human so it became clearer with each passing second. He found himself looking upon a cage with a female witch inside, sitting on the ground as though bored and accepting of her fate.

"What the...?" Axel started, though he couldn't quite process this information. "Hang on!" He yelped as he ran over to test the door and see if he could open it.

"I wouldn't bother trying. Byrne's don't easily let their 'traitor' family members free." The female spat bitterly.

"You're a Byrne?"

The female tilted her head and looked at him with a curious expression. "You know the weight of that?"

"My friend is trying to stop you all."

"Are they?" She chortled a little and rested back against the warm wall. "Well, good luck to them. I'm here waiting for my execution once the war starts."

"Lily's trying to stop the war." Axel commented, making a potentially rash decision. "Right! You're coming with us. You can answer the questions she can't get out of the military liche."

"You've got Luce?!" She roared with laughter for a moment before pushing herself to her feet. "Well, at the very least, I'll come along just to give Luce a good punch in the face."

Axel smirked a little at the idea. For all the times he had seen Lucretia spit at Lily, he would probably enjoy seeing her get punched in the face as well. Reaching out to the hinges of the doors, Axel condensed and focused the air to create pressure inside, building it higher until the bolts couldn't hold anymore and shot across the room.

"I wish they'd have given me such an easy prison to get out of." Axel laughed. Before the woman could say anything more, he pulled the door aside and reached in to grab her frame and throw her over his shoulder.

It didn't take him long to get outside, setting the woman down and running over to where Quinn knelt next to Lily trying to wake her up as Kiki flapped in panicked fear.

~

Hands.

Hands held her. No. Hold wasn't right. They claimed her. They constricted her throat until her mind screamed for oxygen. They pressured her shoulders down and pinned them to solid ground beneath. They caught and restrained her legs when she kicked them out to fight off the hands.

There were so many hands.

"Lily!"

"Lily, come on!"

Blue eyes came into view as she blinked rapidly. Not green eyes, blue. Along with black hair and beard.

"Axel..." Lily rolled over as her body convulsed into a coughing fit, the reality becoming a little clearer. It hadn't been hands on her throat, it was smoke in her lungs making her choke.

"Easy." Axel commented, though the hand rubbing her back was not his. Glancing over her shoulder, she saw a white-haired stranger with blue eyes just as bright as

Axel's. His smile was softer though, reassuring, though he held a much more intimidating aura than Axel did.

"Is that... the fairy Lily?"

"Did she kill the family?"

"Is she here to kill us all?"

The whispers grew in the crowd around them, and Lily could see wands being drawn by those who didn't realise that the different lived among them.

"I... killed...?" She stammered, trying to push herself up without the strength to do so. She wouldn't kill. She didn't want to hurt anyone. She couldn't... could she? She could remember terror but nothing in the reality past that moment Lexi had reached for her throat. Had she killed him? How could she do that? Her breathing quickened as the anxiety and panic spread through her.

"Lily, calm down." The white haired stranger soothed, his hand running over her hair in a manner used to calm children. The heat of the fire had burned away from effects of her water spells which kept her disguise up. Her hair was obviously white, with her skin shimmering beneath the soot and debris.

She heard Axel snap at people to back away. Though the chattering was becoming angrier.

"We should leave." A female voice she didn't recognise spoke.

Who were these people?! How much time had she lost to the hallucinations and memories of things she didn't want to experience?

Spells were sent their way and blocked by the female. Lily's focus blurred as her chest convulsed again. She couldn't fight. She wanted to be at home with her parents. She wished she'd never left. She could be in her warm room with Oscar curled by her belly while Kiki slept by her head. She could wake up and eat fresh fruit and watch her mother do her hair up in fancy braids.

Instead, she hadn't slept in comfort for almost a year now. The voices in her head would not stop. Oscar was no longer there. Her parents may as well be in another world entirely.

Laughter wasn't pure anymore, it was sarcastic or bitter as it followed gallows humour so closely in her life now.

The feel of arms under her and the rhythm of the jog that her holder took rocked her in and out of consciousness.

She just wanted everything to stop.

She didn't want to do this anymore.

Life was not worth the torment. Life was not worth the pain.

Chapter 13: Misha Byrne

The next time she awoke, Lily found herself looking up at the star-dotted sky, her head cradled by a softness she had never known, her body warm and her chest slightly heavy with the vibrating weight of a purring feline.

Lily glanced at Kiki who snored intermittently between the healing purrs. It hadn't all stopped then. Sighing almost in disappointment, Lily turned her eyes back to the quiet sky. Breathing felt like it burned as she turned the hazy memories over in her head.

She'd killed the family? She remembered retaliating with fire. Had she actually used the incantation? She couldn't remember. All she could remember was green eyes and fear.

Reaching up with her right hand, she touched her cheek to realise that tears were gently running down them. How long had she been crying for? Her face felt tight from where other tears had dried previous to these ones.

"You're ok."

Lily tilted her head up until she was looking at the upside-down view of the white-haired stranger looking over his shoulder at her.

"Who are you?" Lily's voice cracked as she spoke.

With a smile, the man reached around to hand her a small container of water. Lily felt pressure on the back of her neck, giving her support as she sat up. It was a tail. A larger, white spotted, fluffy tail.

"Vilankuri?" She asked, looking up at the gentle expression.

"Half. But yes, I'm a large cat like Axel. My name's Quinn, unfortunately, given the name of one of the women you are hunting."

Lily took a sip of the water. It was freezing but it unleashed a desperate thirst in her.

"Steady. You were in that fire for a while. You'll be highly dehydrated." The stranger said, reaching out to slow her pouring speed as she gulped greedily at the water. The more that hit her stomach, the more her stomach seemed to turn. Ok, so this stranger knew what he was talking about.

"Did I… really?" She didn't really want to know the answer, her hand finding Kiki's fur and causing the kitten to stir and looking up at her sleepily.

"It appears they all died in the fire." Quinn confirmed.

"Oh," Lily whimpered as tears pricked her eyes. She was a killer. She hadn't meant to. She would never have meant to. Lily had meant her words to Lucretia when she said she didn't want to hurt anyone.

"They were Byrnes." Axel groggy voice sounded, drawing her eyes over to where he was pushing himself up next to the fire he slept by.

Why did he say that like it made it okay? Lily looked at him with a devastated expression. "So?!"

"So, we needed to stop them."

"Stop them! Not kill them!" Lily shrieked, starling nearby birds into flight.

"They would have killed you the moment they found out who you were." It was the female who had blocked spells aimed at them while Lily couldn't stay conscious.

"I don't want to be the same as them! How is that so hard to understand?!" Lily cried. How could she possibly live with herself if she became someone who could kill and hurt without care?

"You aren't," Kiki chimed, jumping onto her knees to nuzzle away the tears on Lily's cheek. "If you were, you wouldn't feel the pain you are in right now."

Lily scoffed.

"You should have just left me." She grumbled. "I've had enough of everything." Pushing herself to her feet, she walked away from the group. She didn't want to be with them. She didn't want to be anywhere; all the places she craved were no longer options.

Kiki followed but, thankfully, the others gave her space.

"What am I doing, Ki?" Lily whispered sadly. "I want to go home."

"So, let's go home."

Lily turned to raise an eyebrow at the little cat who looked at with empathetic eyes. "What?"

"Let's go home."

"We're banished."

"They'll never expect us to sneak in and spend some time with mum and dad." Kiki winked at the idea. Could they really do that?

"Lily?" Lily sighed at Axel's voice approaching her. Really? She couldn't even get five minutes?! Turning to him with a raised eyebrow, she folded her arms across her chest.

"What, Axel?"

The challenging expression she received was not subtle, but she didn't care. He could be bigger than her, older than her, more powerful than her, whatever... She didn't care.

"This is Misha." He paused. "Misha Byrne."

Lily turned sharp eyes on the female, finally taking her in. She wasn't someone who would stand out in a crowd. She had cropped brown hair and those tell-tale green eyes that seemed to belong to Byrne's more often than not. She was only slightly taller than Lily and the clothes she wore were covered in dust and holes. From Lily's experience, Byrne's were high up in society and therefore well-presented.

"There was no Misha in that family." She commented suspiciously.

Misha laughed bitterly. "Of course not. I went against them, so they got rid of all traces of me and locked me in that hidden room you passed out in."

Lily surveyed her for a minute. "I thought they killed people who rebelled?"

"This close to a war, they were just going to wait and make me a war victim."

"And blame fairies for it?"

"Exactly."

Rage bubbled inside her.

"So, I would like to thank you." Misha continued. "If you hadn't come along, I'd have died in that cage."

Lily blinked at her. She'd killed five people but saved one. The five who died were part of the reason mass genocide continued every hundred years. The one who had been saved stood against it. Did that mean her actions had helped the 'good' of the world?

It still didn't change the fact she had killed people, no matter how unintentionally.

"Lily…" Axel reached out only for her to flinch away. Looking up at him with the shadows of fear in her eyes, she shook her head.

"Please don't touch me." She whispered in a broken voice.

Axel lowered his hand with a look of guilt on his face. The girl in front of him became more broken with every day that passed.

Lily wrapped her arms around her stomach before looking back at Misha with hollow eyes. Misha swallowed before opening her mouth again, a little more cautious this time. "I hear you have Lucretia. If you let me punch her in the face, I'll help you locate every other member of the family?"

Well, that wasn't what Lily had expected.

"Why would you want to punch her?"

"She's the one who sold me out and had me put in that cage." Misha shrugged.

"She did seem the type to do that." Lily sighed. "You know what, do what you want. She's in the satchel." Even if Misha was lying and was just aiming to free Lucretia, honestly, Lily found she couldn't care less.

"You're just going to let me...?"

"You're a witch, right? You can change her back." Lily stated with finality.

"I was more surprised at the trust." Misha admitted.

"It's not trust. I just don't have it in me to care, right now." Lily shrugged, turning away from them and continuing so she could walk away from the two and sit down where she could see the campfire but couldn't hear much.

The peacefulness of the midnight wind was what she needed. Though it didn't quite silence her mind.

Murderer.

Failure.

Useless.

Pathetic.

So many words, so little strength to fight against them.

"We should definitely go home and see mom and dad." Kiki jumped up onto Lily's lap and curled up with that soft, healing purr she excelled at.

"Yeah." Lily whispered, in that moment desperate to curl up in the arms of her parents and beg for forgiveness.

"Oh! She actually did it!" Kiki chimed, guiding Lily's eyes to the sight of Lucretia stumbling backwards from the weight of the blow Misha had landed. "She's got some power for someone not much bigger than you."

"And who has been in a cage for a while." Lily added.

"It might be nice to have some more allies..." Kiki's suggestion was obvious even without her speaking.

"Ki." Lily sighed. "People around me die. It's not wise for them to stay."

"What if they choose to anyway?"

Lily shook her head, looking over the scene of Misha and Lucretia descending into a more vicious fight while Quinn and Axel backed off. They all seemed to have no one else, so maybe they would choose to come with her. But it still wasn't fair. Especially for Axel and Quinn, this war had nothing to do with their kind. They had no loyalty to either side, and no loyalty to Lily.

"I doubt they would." No one seemed to put themselves at risk for 'the right thing'. Lily was beginning to truly believe that she was an idiot for even trying. The whole journey had been nothing but agonising. "I'm not even sure I'm doing the right thing anymore."

"Of course, you are. You said it yourself on the Xeomont Peaks; we can't just walk away knowing how many people will die in a war that is fuelled by a lie." Kiki leant her head against Lily's stomach and nuzzled into her gently. "If we become everything we hate to save everyone else... well, I can't imagine anyone else being kind enough to do it."

"Stupid enough, more like." Lily snorted, raising a hand to block the smack aimed at her by a tiny white paw.

"And," Kiki continued. "If you decide you don't want to do it anymore, I'll be right there with you running to the other side of the world to find peace."

Damn her.

Lily turned a small scowl at the kitten. She was being played like a fiddle and she knew it. They both knew that as soon as Kiki started giving her options that meant she could run away and never face it again would make Lily realise she could never do that. The guilt she would live with would be unbearable. This pain was terrifying, it was immobilising at times, but it was layered with enough anger that it kept her on her feet.

Her pain, Lily could live with. Others pain was not.

"Ok." Lily sighed, her mind settling on the only conclusion. She had to see it through.

Wrapping her arms around the kitten as she got to her feet, Lily walked back over to the campfire. Her heart was heavy and her stomach hollow, but her steps were solid.

"Alright, enough." She said as she drew closer, raising a hand and reciting the incantation to turn Lucretia back into a mouse. Quinn caught her with quick reflexes and placed her back in the cage as Lily continued. "I'm going back to Fae Greenwood."

"I thought you were banished?" Axel asked in confusion.

"I am." Lily confirmed. "But I'm going back anyway. Not only do I want to see my parents, but there's Byrne's in there which I need to find."

"Cyrus too," Kiki added.

"Which may not go well." Lily shrugged. "I don't want to ask anyone to come with me. It's safer if you don't."

"And what if 'safe' isn't something I'm worried about having?" Axel challenged with a smirk.

"Then, you are a strange man." Lily replied.

"Ok, so you can walk unsafe roads and not be strange?"

Lily's lips twitched into a small smile which grew into a cheeky smirk. "I've always been strange."

"Well, get used to not being the only one." Axel laughed.

Rolling her eyes with a slight fondness in her expression, Lily turned to look at the other two.

"As a Byrne, I doubt you are just going to let me go?" Misha raised an eyebrow. She had a point. Lily didn't know if she was really against the war. It could all be another elaborate lie to gain her trust and make sure she failed.

Misha wasn't Finnigan.

She was still a Byrne.

Could Lily really just discriminate based on trust issues and heritage? Did that make her just as bad as everyone else following the beliefs of the past?

"You're right. I can't just let you walk away." Lily said. "I don't know if you are really against this war. I don't know if you are going to be trustworthy or not."

"But..." she continued. "I want to believe it. I don't want to automatically distrust everyone because of Finnigan. If you don't want to be involved, I would ask you to let me turn you into an animal I can keep in the satchel when I'm not with you."

Misha chortled at the idea and shook her head. "So long as you make me bigger than Luce so I can be in charge, I don't mind being an animal. However, if you can trust me to an extent, I can help you identify the rest of the Byrne family."

Now that would be a huge help. It would certainly save time too.

"You'd sell them all out?"

"And tell you which ones are actually against the war but too scared of being killed to say it openly."

"There's more of you?"

"Just because we're related to greedy psychopaths, doesn't mean we are all the same." Misha deadpanned, making Lily flush in embarrassment.

"Of course, sorry."

"One of my cousins, Yuri, has been subtly undermining the fairies' beliefs for centuries. Unfortunately, most of the people she can convince get too loud about it and end up getting arrested."

"Wait," Quinn interrupted. "There's already unrest in the fairies."

"And the witches."

"What?!" Lily exclaimed. "Who?"

"There's plenty out there who don't want to fight and kill. It's just they can't make any bridges without going missing and they end up believing the other side is to blame." Misha explained. "Any time the family catches wind of rebellion, they send the family members of the other race to get rid of the threat."

"Which would only enhance the distrust and anger," Quinn concluded.

"Exactly." Misha nodded.

"So, theoretically, with the Byrne's not around, we should be able to build bridges?" Lily asked.

"There's a lot of others who would squash those attempts as well. Those who survived wars and lost people. Those who truly believe the history books." Misha sighed. "It won't be as simple as cutting out the source of the rot."

"It's still a good place to start," Quinn countered, sending a reassuring smile to Lily as though he knew her mind had begun to be overwhelmed by the scale of her goal again. It grew faster than she could keep up. Though, it did cause a fine white eyebrow to raise on her forehead towards him.

"You're coming too?"

Quinn nodded. "Axel told me what you were really aiming to do. The war has gone on far too long, so yes, I will help."

"Huh,"

"You don't believe me?"

"No one helps just because; even Axel's doing it for the thrill."

"Hey!" Axel protested.

"You saying you aren't?" Lily challenged.

"Well, it's a factor." Axel flushed a little and folded his arms across his chest. It only really dawned on Lily now that both he and Quinn looked fully human aside from the feline ears on their heads and the tails which hung from the base of their spines.

"It might be easier for you to sneak in if you are both in animal form? Though you'll still be a bit too big." Lily thought aloud. "Maybe you should stay on the ground in the woods."

"We've got some distance to travel before that so we can plan on the way." Misha offered.

"It is a long walk." Kiki agreed.

"On human legs maybe," Axel chortled, looking at Quinn with a glint in his eye. "Us big cats can travel much greater distances in the same amount of time."

"Talk about riding in style!" Misha laughed.

"Ok. So how about we head for the Densewood then along to the Greenwood?" Quinn suggested. "It'll be longer but we'll be less likely to catch anyone's attention. Lily, are you going to be ok to ride?"

They all glanced at her, or rather, at the dryness of her skin, the still-cracking sound of her voice from lungs infected with smoke, and at the bruises around her throat where she had been lifted by Alexander.

"I'll be fine." Lily straightened her back as she spoke. It would be her mantra going forward. No matter what, she would be... 'fine'.

Chapter 14: Back Home

'Fine' was a word that often didn't mean what it was supposed to. As the days went by, Lily insisted she was 'fine'; when she woke up from nightmares, when she flinched from someone reaching out to her when she wasn't expecting it, when she scratched at the scars the handcuffs had left on her wrists, when her throat closed up at the memory of shackles there, when she cried herself to sleep at night over the fact she had ended lives.

She was fine.

She had to be fine.

If she wasn't, what other option did she have? Give up? Hand herself over? Die?

Lily didn't care for the jests and the banter that occurred whenever the little group stopped for rest or food.

She was quiet. No. She was borderline silent. And once again, any time she was asked if she was ok she said that word: 'fine'.

It was a lie, of course. Lily was anything but fine. She was scared of the world and herself. She was upset and shamed and angry. She felt like she was numb while her nerves were on fire at the same time. She was alert and conscious of everything around her and yet on the same hand she spaced out and was lost in her own mind.

If it wasn't for Misha sitting next to her and placing the food in her hands with a little bit of force, Lily may not have eaten either. Hunger was vanishing from her body as quickly as humour was.

And that was the scariest of all the things.

Lily only had the motivation to keep physically moving, but if she got taken out in the process she didn't think she would mind. She could keep going knowing she was doing it for others, but she was tired, so very exhausted both mentally and emotionally.

"Whoa! This place is gorgeous!" Quinn breathed as they passed the threshold between the Archaic Densewood and the Fae Greenwood. It instantly went from dark and ominous to well-lit wood floors and colours of all kinds blooming in the forms of flowers and fruits. The trees were deep greens that would indicate the height of spring.

How long had Lily been away? She had left in the fall to go to the witches' world... but so much had happened. It couldn't have been only a year and a half. Had it been more than two? Was she seventeen now? Nearly eighteen?

Glancing around, the white-haired girl felt a lack of warmth compared to what she knew from her home. Even if it hadn't been friendly, the sun always warmed her skin. Right now, it wasn't doing anything. Was that her being numb or was something going on in the woods?

Lily felt even more like a stranger than she ever had done before.

"It's always gorgeous to look at," Kiki sighed. Her mood had been simultaneously dropping along with Lily's. "It's not full of the best people though."

"The whole world seems to be like that." Misha shrugged. "So, the plan is Lily sneaks in to see her parents with me disguised as a little song bird so I can identify any Byrnes if I see them?"

"And we patrol the ground just to make sure you guys get away fine." Axel agreed.

"If we make it back here. I can't blend in here." Lily warned them. "Nothing can create the wings I don't have."

If anyone knew that it was her, she had tried everything she could think of.

Axel reached out to ruffle her hair, approaching from the front so she had time to do something other than glare if she wanted to. Lily didn't. And this time, because she had seen the movement, she didn't flinch either.

"You got this." Axel grinned at her like a mischievous older brother.

"Thanks. Look after these." Handing over the satchel and her scythe, Lily both felt uneasy leaving them, but if anyone was going to keep them away from the wrong hands, it was someone who didn't have a loyalty to either side.

Heh, even Lily disliked how she had to back up any small amount of trust with logical arguments for it. Blind trust just seemed like too much of a risk these days.

Turning back to Misha, Lily raised her hand and incited *"nilamjai svica"* to transform her into a beautiful blue jay who would fit in with the many blue jays that became companions in the fairy world. No one would bat an eye. Nodding her beaked-head, Misha tested out the wings by fluttering up to a few branches and then back down onto Lily's satchel where she peaked tauntingly at the cage inside, causing Lucretia to squeal in annoyance.

"Misha..." Quinn chortled. The blue jay gave him a look that screamed false innocence before flying to perch herself on Lily's shoulder. Quinn's ice blue eyes met Lily's. "Be careful. We'll protect the documents."

"Thanks." Lily whispered to both the men. They were under one of the trees in the outskirts of the kingdom, she had to make it a long way into the centre to be able to find her parents' house.

"Are you sure we shouldn't wait until dark?" Kiki asked.

"No," Lily shook her head. "That'll be the most obvious time to be defensive when a war is coming up. In the daylight, people will be doing their usual daily routines and working on automatic. Much less likely to notice something."

"Besides," she continued. "We spent every exploration of the woods trying to do it with as few people seeing us as possible, so we know the best routes for the day."

"Good point."

Lily smiled softly, scratching the cat behind her left ear. "Let's go."

Infiltrating the fairy kingdom was the easiest thing she had done so far. Lily knew where the works occurred and she knew where the home districts were. She knew the trees with more foliage that she could use to hide her from sight and she knew which trees were built inside so she could use those to her advantage.

By sundown, she found herself outside of the window of her old bedroom. Placing her hand against the panes, she melted the ice-glass and slid inside before reforming it back into place.

The sound of her parents' voices filtered through the house, her father making her mother laugh nearly bringing Lily to tears. How long had it been since she heard that?

Should she really be here? She was putting them at risk by coming back to see them. Kiki nudged the back of her leg gently, encouraging her to step out of the bedroom she had grown up with.

"Who's there?!" the voice of her father's companion called from the kitchen. The boots Lily wore weren't as silent as her feet it would seem. "Show yourself!"

Why was Lily scared? Why was she hesitating? Her parents wouldn't judge her for what she had been doing, would they? Lily let out a shuddering breath and stepped into the kitchen doorway and locked eyes on the sight of her parents more than ready for a fight.

Time stood still.

It was clear the last thing they had ever expected was for their daughter to be in their house.

"Lily?" Isa breathed.

"Hey." Lily whispered back.

Her parents had never moved as fast as they did crossing the kitchen and throwing their arms around their daughter. They didn't engulf her like they used to. Lily had grown in height and filled out in body since leaving. But that didn't stop their arms feeling like the safest place, the only place she could burst into tears and cling to them as if her life depended on it.

Terra brushed Lily's hair back, pausing as her hand ran over the burned side which was still refusing to grow any hair back.

"Oh sweetie, what's happened?" She soothed, kissing Lily's head as Isa took her weight. Lily felt completely weak, her legs didn't want to hold her up and her breathing was ragged as the tears became more unhinged.

"It's ok, darling." Isa whispered to her. "You're safe."

Was she though? Her parents couldn't keep her safe from herself any more than they had been able to protect her from banishment. They didn't know anything; how could they promise her security?

Shaking her head, she pulled back from their hold and moved to sit herself at the breakfast bench.

"I'm not safe. I doubt I ever will be." Lily stated, wiping her tears aside.

"Of course, you can be. You can settle down somewhere away from here." Terra said.

"Mom, you have no idea how much is out there…"

"No, but that must mean there would be a safe place somewhere!" Lily thought of Kita-Utara. It was certainly possible to live under the radar. Or she could go and find out if the 'mainland' that Kipar had spoken of was real and find somewhere to call home.

"But this war has to be stopped."

"What? Why?" Isa asked, reminding Lily that she had never had the chance to explain what she had discovered to them before she had been banished. As she began to explain, it became very obvious she would have been better off bringing her satchel of evidence with her.

The look of disbelief was unmissable from all faces aside from Kiki's.

"That… sounds incredibly unlikely, Lil." Isa began.

"It's real!" She insisted.

Isa and Terra looked to one another before sighing softly. Terra pulled away and headed over to their food cupboard to fetch fresh fruit for Lily to eat.

"You need to get some rest, sweetie." Isa half instructed as Lily took the fruit and bit into it with a sigh of relief. All the fruit and food she had been able to grow herself over the past moons had never been this sweet.

"Your father's right." Terra agreed. "We can talk about this more tomorrow."

With both of their gentle faces and the safety of the walls she had grown up in, Lily felt the exhaustion of the last year or more crash against her like a tidal wave. Like an adrenaline crash on a colossal scale, she could almost feel her legs want to give out under her at the promise of a safe place to rest.

Just because she was home, didn't mean she was going to be safe from the nightmares that plagued her. That thought was almost enough to make her refuse the arm that guided her to her old room.

It hadn't changed in the slightest. Lily could have sworn she had seen Oscar curled at the side of her pillow the moment she opened the door, but a blink later confirmed she was imagining things.

"Lil?" Isa prompted as Lily hesitated in the doorway.

"Feels... wrong. Being here without Oscar." She whispered. Feeling her father's arms wrap around her, she leant into his strength and sighed shakily.

"Oscar's still in your heart, he's never going to be truly gone."

Lily closed her eyes at the sentiment. Her parents didn't know; they couldn't even imagine how it felt to have a part of yourself die. They couldn't know how it left a hollow part of you that could never be filled and would always ache like a phantom limb. The ever present feeling that something was wrong and something was missing would haunt her body and mind for the rest of her days. No amount of time or mission was helping it get any easier and she doubted it ever would.

Lily figured there was a lot her parents wouldn't understand. And, right now, she was too tired to push it. So, she smiled sadly before pulling off her boots and climbing into the bed she had spent so many years using.

A duvet had never felt so cold.

Kiki crawled under the material and curled up against Lily's stomach. "They'll listen more in the morning." She whispered, though her voice betrayed the level of doubt she had in her own words. She would never have believed it before being in the witches world for as long as she had been. Or, would she? If Lily had a child, she liked to think that she would believe them enough to look further into it as well.

Falling into a troubled sleep, Lily found that even the comfort of her childhood home couldn't keep her from her nightmares. Binds. Chains. Green eyes. Laughter. Powerlessness.

By the time her parents emerged for breakfast, Lily had been sitting at the kitchen counter for hours with Kiki's forehead resting against her own and her fingers fiddling with the ends of her hair.

"Couldn't sleep?" Terra asked, softly pressing her lips to Lily's temple.

"Sleep hasn't been my friend since I left Mythanissiam." Lily admitted.

"You need a break."

"How am I supposed to take a break? I'm not welcome anywhere safe enough to rest." Lily sighed and shook her head. "Besides, there's a war that's imminent that could be stopped if the Byrnes weren't here fuelling the fires."

"One family can't be the cause for this much divide between races." Isa countered.

"They started it, and they make sure it continues." Lily grumbled. "They leave no room for anyone to think about a peace between everyone."

"Witches have been killing us for our wings for centuries, Lily." Terra said in exasperation. "No single family could convince a whole race they needed our wings."

"They don't use our wings!" Lily rolled her eyes. "'Fae wings' are wings from creatures called Karai."

"Well of course they'd tell you that."

"I saw them!" Lily raised her voice. "I was thought to be a witch and I saw the ingredients known as Fae Wings. They were not from a fairy!"

"Lily..."

"Why is it so hard to believe me?!" Lily felt annoyance, frustration and pain build up within her. "Why would I lie about anything?"

"Are you sure you aren't just reading into it? Maybe being a little sensitive because of Finnigan?" Terra suggested gently.

Lily looked at her incredulously. "I've based most of this conclusion against many things other than Finnigan Byrne." Lily said. "And if I'm sensitive about him it's because not only did he lie to me for ages, but he tied me down, took my magic from me, left me to die, attempted to kill me twice and actually killed Oscar!"

Lily raised a hand to silence her parents before they could speak again, her frustration morphing into the hopeless anger she was beginning to know intimately. "This isn't about him, anyway! This is about how many people die pointlessly."

"Even if it's true, this isn't your fight." Isa sighed.

"Then whose fight is it?" Lily demanded.

"Lil, you're just a kid." Terra attempted to reach out to her daughter, only to be shaken off.

"I've been through more than you could ever imagine." Lily snarled.

"Don't talk to your mother that way." Isa snapped. "Our races have been at war since forever, there's no chance of stopping something that big and you are being stupid if you think you could."

What was going on? She'd come here for support and somehow, she was becoming the scolded child. Why were her own parents taking the same stance as the Dregana? How could they be so closed to the idea of change?

"Life is good here Lily. Why would you ever want to change it?" Terra interjected. "The witches are foul. How can you possibly be on their side after what they've done to you?"

"Because it wasn't witches in general!"

"You said they were all on alert and hunting you."

"Yes, because they think fairies are evil."

"Of course, they would spin it like that!" Isa raised his voice for the first time that Lily could remember. "They are manipulating you."

"We are all being manipulated!" Lily snapped.

"Enough!" Terra yelled. "Lily. You do not understand. I may not have lived through a war yet, but I heard all the stories from your grandparents. Witches are savages."

"They are just like us!"

"Stop Lily! You have been deluded!" Terra snapped, silencing the teenager in surprise.

"No." Lily spoke quietly but steadily. "I'm the only one seeing clearly."

"Just because you are different, doesn't mean the whole world is wrong!" Lily recoiled at the words from her mother. "I'm sorry you were born wrong, but you can't just demand the world to change to suit you."

"Born wrong?" Lily repeated with a broken heart. "Is that what you guys really think?"

"No, we love you." Isa placed his hand on his wife's shoulder to keep her calm. "We just wanted so much more for you."

"I've done everything I can…"

"You should be happy, settling down and having a family. But without wings no one was going to have you as a wife in case their kids were wingless too." Terra teared up as though this was something that hurt her more than the white-haired girl in front of her.

"I've never even thought about kids."

"If we'd done better, or raised you differently, you might have done. And you wouldn't have had to go through all this and suffer so badly."

Lily scowled even with the tears in her eyes. "And I might have been completely miserable and died in a pointless war."

She'd honestly heard enough. Coming here was a mistake. It was unearthing things even her mind hadn't whispered to her. Even in the eyes of her parents, she wasn't actually good enough. They didn't believe in her words. No. They didn't believe in **her**.

"Where are you going?" Isa grabbed her arm to stop her as Lily turned away.

Lily ripped her arm free and refused to look back at them.

"To prove you wrong."

With that, she exited the front door and dropped down on a vine until she reached the woodland ground floor and threw up shadows to hide her from sight.

The fluttering of small wings indicated Kiki and Misha's presence even before they located her in the dark Lily kept steady to prevent her parents following her or other fairies spotting her. Misha had been flitting around the neighbourhood checking in on windows in case she could spot a Byrne; she must have seen Lily burst out of the front door which certainly had not been the plan.

Changing her back to her human form, Lily spoke to Misha. "Did you find anyone?"

"Lily, we don't…"

"Did you find anyone?" Lily spoke sternly over Kiki. She wasn't doing this now. She wasn't going to share her pain with Misha who could still possibly be here to trick and use her.

"Bianca and Silas." Misha confirmed. "They live a few branches over from you apparently. I think Silas is Bianca's father?"

"We'll start there."

"What are you going to do?" Misha asked, almost wary of the distant tone in Lily's voice.

"Have them join Lucretia for now, you can fly them back to the guys and put them in the cage."

"You know, I could help get rid of them?" Misha offered.

"No." Lily snapped. "I don't want anyone else to die." She couldn't... she wouldn't let it happen. "I will work something out eventually."

Misha gave her a look filled with scepticism but shrugged in submission. "Your choice. Am I being a blue jay? Or can I have my wand to back you up?"

Back-up sounded good. But... to be inside the walls of a Byrne home with three Byrnes seemed too big a risk, even if one of them wanted her to believe she was an ally. The smile of Finnigan flashed through her mind from all those times he had held his hand out to her in support. He had lied for so long. There was a good chance that Misha was cut from the same cloth.

"Sorry." Lily whispered as she sent the transmutation spell at Misha once more. She couldn't do it. She couldn't let herself trust the woman. And Lily hated herself for it.

Waiting for nightfall, Lily decided to push forward. She made her way back up into the tree. Following Misha to the branch in question, Lily repeated her actions to get inside, removing the window but this time keeping the water floating around her wrists ready to freeze as shields if need be.

She motioned for Kiki to stay back, knowing she was more likely to get hurt than do damage. Plus, Lily would not survive if she lost the little feline as well.

"Bianca! Hurry up!" A male voice called through the house. "You know your grandad doesn't like to be kept waiting!"

"Grandpa Cy needs to chill!" A younger female voice replied as footsteps approached the room.

"We're supposed to be initiating Jared, we don't have time for faffing about!"

Lily cast a look at Kiki. She'd been right… Jared was a Byrne. And if they followed these two, they would find Cyrus. Slipping back out of the window and replacing the ice panes before the door opened, Lily flattened her against the outside of the branch, her fingers digging into the bark so she didn't lose grip.

"You can't be serious!" Kiki hissed.

"How else are we going to find Cyrus?!" Lily demanded back in the quietest voice she could muster.

"But there will be too many Byrnes to deal with!"

"We don't have a choice!" The fairy and feline stared each other down until Kiki clicked her tongue in annoyance and backed down.

"You're being reckless." Kiki hissed to deaf ears. Lily didn't care. This was likely the only chance she had to have someone physically lead her to one of the origins of this huge lie. She glanced at Kiki before nodding her head towards the front of the house where the door was closed behind the exiting fairies.

Following people was considerably more difficult than just hiding from everyone. You had to keep the target in sight while staying out of their attention. When you couldn't fly straight like them, it meant a lot of hopping from branch to branch with vines holding onto your wrists and ice forming in the air to be used as steps.

They clearly didn't expect anyone to be onto them. Not once did either fairy look around to check if they were being followed. But then, who would follow them? They were a father and daughter out for a night time fly, it wasn't strange. They flew lower than most fairies would go though, following the main trunk until they were almost at the magic barrier. Only then did they stop, Silas placing his hand against the bark and forcing an opening to grow.

Of course.

It seemed obvious that Cyrus would be hidden away right in the centre of the kingdom where it wouldn't be odd for people to visit.

Landing in the opening behind the two, Lily raised her hands to grab one shoulder from each. *"Tikusoma Svica"*. They barely had time to turn around before both were on the ground squeaking in anger and confusion. "Take them back to Axel and Quinn." Lily looked at Kiki, clearly giving this task to her.

"I'm not going to leave you."

"Exactly. I can't lose you." Lily swallowed the stone growing in her throat at the thought. "I need to know you are ok, Ki. Please."

Kiki clicked her tongue again but sighed and dove down to catch the two mice scrambling down the hallway. With one in her front paws and the other held in her mouth, Kiki left through the opening and disappeared into the twilight darkness.

Perhaps she should have sent Misha with the feline, but it seemed better to keep an eye on all Byrnes that weren't caged as mice. Motioning for the blue jay to follow, Lily stepped cautiously through the hallway, no, it was more like a tunnel. There were no doorways or turnings, just one long tunnel on a slight upward slope to the other side of the tree.

Chapter 15: Cyrus Byrne

"Where are Silas and Bianca?" A familiar voice floated through the tunnel. Layla Linwood was already here.

"Forget it. They shall face consequences later." A cold voice replied. One Lily didn't recognise even slightly. Was that Cyrus? "We have more important matters."

"That we do. Jared..." Another unknown voice. Creeping closer to the door at the end of the tunnel, Lily found herself gazing through the gap that had been left open. Jared stood in the centre of the room looking confused and concerned while he was flanked by his mother on one side and the ice council elder on the other. In front, stood a water fairy of towering height, and a wingless male... with dark purple hair? Since when did fairies or witches have purple hair?!

Wait...

Pyran had purple hair without it being due to his race. Had Cyrus been born under the influence of the Morequacor? Did that mean he had abilities over the mind? It would make sense, to be able to convince all the right people of the same story for centuries... there was surely more involved than just discriminatory history telling.

A sudden jolt of fear ran through Lily, did this mean he was about to brainwash Jared?!

Focusing on the goings-on inside the door, Lily attempted to catch up on the information which Jared was being given. The way Cyrus spoke was like a commander giving a briefing to someone who was not allowed to question the way of things. He was straight forward, cold and somewhat smug. He didn't seem remotely bothered by the fact Jared's expression shifted from confusion to disbelief to horrified disgust as the reality of the story settled in.

"You mean... no one actually has to die?" Jared whispered.

"Of course, they have to die." Layla snapped.

"If our bloodline is to thrive and continue in power, some lower lives must be sacrificed." Cyrus explained.

"Lower lives?" Jared repeated, his skin turning sickly green under the dark shimmer. His feathered wings curled in around him as though trying to protect him from what he was hearing. "I don't think anyone's life is lower than mine."

Lily felt a swell of respect in her chest at those words. That was the Jared she knew from her childhood, the boy who would help her even though she was the outcast of the community. She also felt dread in her stomach as Misha ruffled her wings in discomfort. Both of them knew what fate Jared would meet if he refused to go along with the family.

"You will have to learn to accept it if you are to be in this family, Jared." The water-fairy spoke as the ice elder placed her hand on the boy's shoulder.

"I can't."

"If you don't, you will die." Cyrus warned, his meaning obvious even without the way his hand raised to aim his hand towards the teen in threat. Lily cast her eyes downward. Was she going to lose someone else good from her life?

"I'd rather die than be the reason so many lose their lives." Lily looked up again at the words that came, they were more confident than she had ever heard Jared speak and, when she looked through the gap in the door, her eyes locked with his.

Lily froze.

He knew she was there; his eyes were full of recognition.

"Son, you don't know what you are talking about." Layla spoke, drawing Jared's dark eyes away from Lily and up to his mother.

"Yes, I do. I've never agreed with the way you treat people." Jared continued to speak with solid confidence, shaking off the hand on his shoulder and stepping away from them. "You've always acted like you are superior, yet the best person I ever met was the wingless girl you branded a traitor. Let me guess, she knew about all this, that's why you arrested her immediately when she came back."

"She is a traitor."

"This family is the traitorous one!" Jared snapped, stepping towards the door.

"If you leave, you will die." Cyrus turned to follow Jared with his eyes.

"So, kill me!" Jared dared, walking more determinedly towards the only exit he could see. The moment Cyrus tensed his hand and opened his mouth to speak a spell, Lily barged through the door and threw herself between him and Jared.

"*Addari!*" She yelled while her arms drew up to cross each other and protect her face instinctively. The barrier she created was around herself and the force of the spell sent her reeling off to the side of the room and through the wall with a vicious crack of bark.

The barrier remained around her long enough to take the brunt of the fall, but it didn't stop Lily's head colliding with the floor at an unhealthy speed.

Groaning in pain, Lily raised her hand to investigate any damage. There was already a lump, and if the warmth and damp was anything to go by, she was bleeding.

"You stupid child! You cannot stop us." Cyrus descended from above on a charmed rug. He knew incantation magic like any witch.

Lowering her hand, ignoring the blood that stained her fingertips, Lily pushed herself to her feet. "I have to try."

"No one can stand against death." Cyrus laughed ominously, raising his left hand which Lily noticed was bound in a metallic accessory. It twisted around his middle finger like a ring then connected to more metal which twisted around half his forearm. It glowed the same foreboding violet as the man's eyes.

A heavy thudding sounded in the distance.

What was that?

Whatever it was, it was huge.

The foliage of trees to the right parted to show the skull head of the Macellavir. This wasn't a mirage. This was breaking branches and crushing undergrowth with every movement.

"But... that's a myth."

"Because I made it so..."

Lily gulped, trying to calm her heightened breathing and think of anything other than terror when looking at the beast which towered over her.

Wait, there was another skull further down? And the rotten vines covered a vast area but the feet that could be seen briefly with each step were only the size of a large elk.

"What?"

"I'd still run if I were you even if it's not exactly what the stories tell you. It is still death." Cyrus clicked his fingers and motioned towards the young fairy. Sure enough, everything around the creature was dying as it stepped too close.

"How have you managed this?" Lily yelped, jumping back to put some distance between her and the large rotten arm that swung and crashed into the floor where she had stood.

"I managed to trick one legend, the Morequacor, into gaining some of its power and now, I control legends of my own! Stupid horse didn't even see it coming."

Lily raised up a shield of ice to brace the foot that swung slow but powerful towards her, knowing she could not outrun it. Shattering the ice, the impact sent Lily flying into a tree trunk with a loud scream of pain leaving her lips.

"This beast has killed anyone who has taken it too far against us, but this is probably my favourite kill." Cyrus sounded almost gleeful at the idea.

Lily coughed trying to recover from the winding she had received. Lifting her head, Lily noticed a twinkle in the grass just within reach. The necklace her parents had made her. It seemed so long ago now. Straining her arm to reach out and grab the trinket, Lily pushed herself to her feet to face the beast which walked toward her, a low growling exuding from behind the visible skulls.

She couldn't give up and leave her parents in the community of someone with this under his control.

"Lily! Catch!"

Spinning around to see Kiki flying toward her with the scythe she had masked as a wand in her paws. Dropping the item for Lily to catch with her free hand, Kiki dove for the Macellavir, scratching at its eyes and making it rear up and howl in anger.

Lily cast *'Addari'* on the scythe before holding it in front of her to block a swipe of rotten vines the beast wielded like a whip.

"*Praeligo!*" Lily cast the binding spell she had read on the parchment of offensive spells, rendering the Macellavir frozen in its attempt to swipe Kiki out of the air. The resistance knocked Lily to the side as the beast broke her hold.

How was she ever meant to stop that?!

Slamming the base of the scythe to the ground she shot vines up to tie around the beast's legs while water pulled from the air froze and assaulted it from all angles. No matter how they pierced it, it didn't stop moving, nor did it bleed. And each vine was ripped out of the ground with ease as rot ate away at them quicker than Lily could encourage the growth.

Shadow engulfed them all and feline snarls sounded before ice shot up from the ground to bind the beast's feet and a gust of wind knocked the beast off balance.

Taking the advantage, Lily forced her legs to move, running in the direction she knew Cyrus had been in. Sure enough, she collided with him. Getting her hands against his head, she focused her concentration and yelled, *"Manac"*

He fought back, Lily had never expected there to be so much pain involved, but she felt like her head might split open. It felt like the pressure was making her head wound worse, like there were hands attempting to crack her skull open like one would a coconut. But soon, Cyrus' body went limp and the Macellavir stopped attacking blindly.

"Give me the armlet." Lily commanded, struggling against the resistance even while watching Cyrus reach across to his arm and unhook the controlling trinket in order to hand it over.

"What are you going to do?" Kiki asked, fluttering down onto her shoulder.

"Stay." Lily growled at the man before standing up and pulling the armlet onto her wrist.

The shadow faded away and she saw Axel limping away from the Macellavir while Quinn stood between them growling and poised for attack. Jared was looking at her with a hardened expression and red eyes as though he had been crying.

"Your mother…?" Lily began, cutting herself off as Jared shook his head.

"She won't be in anyone's way now." Flinching in surprise, Lily looked up to see the Ice Elder drifting to the floor. "Nor will Oakley, I just took care of him."

Lily blinked. The Ice Elder was Yuri? The one who was working to undermine Cyrus in the fairy community? But, she was the one who had banished Lily. Looking at Jared, she felt her heart tighten for him. Even if her parents were against her, she could never wish to see them dead. "I'm sorry." She whispered.

"She wanted so many to die. She… she's lived long enough." He responded with a voice that said he was clearly holding back a lot of emotions.

Not being sure what to say, Lily turned to the Macellavir. Pulling the armlet from her arm, she placed it on the floor, flash burning it with *'agora'* and light magic until it disintegrated. Lily looked up and watched the Macellavir dismantle itself into five individual creatures. Two deer, three wolves, each with skulls for faces. Her eyebrow raised in question but there was no time to ponder anything before the beasts charged in her direction.

Yelping in fear, Lily raised her hand to summon vines to lift her out of the way. However, the beasts were not interested in her. They raced over to where Cyrus remained completely still under Lily's control. He couldn't even scream when their fangs ripped into his flesh.

"Oh..." Lily whimpered at the sight of them devouring the body. She could hear Misha's bird form retching at the sight and smell. They made short work of it before vanishing into the trees. Lily dropped to the ground and glanced at what was left of Cyrus; there wasn't enough to bother seeing if he might have survived.

That was no way to die.

"What in the name of liche were they?" Jared asked pulling Lily's mind away from the sympathy she was feeling for the man who had killed so many.

"Whatever they are, they aren't a problem now." Axel grumbled, changing forms into the fur covered human Lily knew well. Though Jared was almost as concerned about his sudden appearance as he had been with the Macellavir. He glanced from Axel, to the snow leopard and the blue jay. Before he could speak, Lily changed Misha back into her human form while Quinn took on his.

"Lily, you live a very odd life now..." He commented, drawing a tired laugh from the white-haired girl.

"Tell me about it." Lily scoffed. "You wouldn't believe half of the things I've seen."

"Tell me?" Jared's voice was surprisingly gentle as he walked over to Cyrus and examined him.

Looking between the group, Lily wondered if she should just tell them everything. Were they worth the risk of trusting? Jared had been the only person in their community to ever help her outside of her family. He'd just silenced his own mother. Axel, Quinn and Misha had been helping her without any benefit for themselves, and if the Ice Elder really was against the war, it would be good to have everyone on the same page.

Nodding, Lily began to tell her story from her view, walking over to Cyrus and, like she had done to bury Oscar, she pulled his body under the surface of the ground with the use of vines.

"I had wondered where Oscar was." Jared breathed as the story came to an end. Without warning, he had closed the space between them and wrapped his arms around her, burying her face into his chest.

Since when was Jared so tall?

"I'm so sorry Lily." He whispered into her hair as a couple of choked sobs left her throat in the safe darkness of his chest. Looking over her head at her companions, he offered him a smile. "Thank you for being with her since then."

"I'm here for fun." Axel shrugged.

"You just wounded yourself protecting her." Jared pointed out with a raised eyebrow causing Axel to huff and stalk a little way into the woods while Quinn and Misha snickered at him.

Jared shook his head and pulled back from Lily to look her in the eye. "What do we do now?"

"Now? I don't know. No matter where I go I'm the enemy, so I can't convince anyone of anything. You might be able to, now that I've got the Byrnes out of the fairy kingdom?"

"Everyone believes it so firmly. They are terrified of the enemy." Yuri sighed.

"But witches aren't the enemy." Lily said for what felt like the millionth time in her life.

"It's difficult to stop seeing that when it's the only threat you know." Quinn interjected.

He had a point.

"What if there's a bigger one?" Lily breathed, gaining confused looks. Without the main drives of the wars there was still fear, but with something else to fight against... Perhaps the war could be averted. The enemy of my enemy is my friend. That's how the saying went, right.

"Jared. This is going to sound crazy, but you and Yuri need to convince the fairies to escape the woodland. Go north to the mountains and meet with Xalina and Tanith. Take this so they know you are telling the truth." Lily instructed, handing him the necklace still in her hand.

"What are you talking about?" Jared argues.

Lily insists "We are never going to cross boundaries with everyone so kept apart."

Jared needed to become a member of the next council even if he was young. Between him and Yuri, they knew the truth and could have the power to make people think differently.

"Side with Draconians, and when the time comes, side with the witches. Fight the common enemy."

"What common enemy?" Jared interrupted.

"Me."

Stunned silence was broken only by the woodland life in the trees and undergrowth.

"What are you doing?" Kiki broke the silence first.

"Becoming a bigger enemy than the war. They all turn their attention to stopping me, they work together, they realise the wars don't need to happen."

"Lily, that's insane. You'll be killed." Misha protested.

"Maybe, but if everyone fights with each other to do that it'll be worth it. Axel can help make me seem more powerful, and I'm going to hunt down the Morequacor. It made the mistake of giving Cyrus such power, it can make up for it now."

"That's too much risk. Come home." Jared shook his head.

"Jared, listen, not a single race trusts me." Lily stood her ground. "I've escaped places and escaped death many times; I've had part of my soul killed, I've been banished by my people, put in chains by my friends, and probably brought shame on my family. I've appeared in towns and members of communities have disappeared or died. You can blame your mother and Oakley on me as well. I'm already a villain, I just need to become one that is loud about it. Not one in the shadows, but one that needs to be stopped right this moment."

"But…" Quinn stopped speaking as Lily raised a hand to him.

"Please. I have very little left to bother living for. At least, this way, maybe all of you and others I care for get to live in peace."

Jared sighed at the determination in Lily's eyes. She was a different person than the girl he had known before. That girl had barely been able to look him in the face, let alone hold his gaze until he backed down and agreed.

"You've really grown." He mumbled.

"You're one to talk." She teased, motioning at how he towered over her these days.

"You know what I meant." He rolled his eyes and gave her a playful shove. Lily couldn't help but chortle, she did know what he meant, but she still didn't feel grown.

"How are we going to convince everyone to leave?" Yuri asked after a moment.

"I'm going to start a fire." Lily stated. "Axel, Quinn, Misha, can you help spread and control it so no one gets harmed but the trees aren't safe anymore."

"You're going to destroy your home?" Quinn queried.

"I'm going to destroy a place. My home is my parents and my friends, and I'm trying to save them."

"Touché." Axel saluted her.

"We can certainly control it for you." Misha agreed as Lily took her wand from the satchel and handed it back to her. She'd earned that much trust.

"Thank you."

Turning back to Jared, Lily smiled softly. "Go. Tell them I killed your mother and that I'm intent on destroying a place that never made me feel welcome. Oakley, Silas, and Bianca can be 'collateral damage'. Tell them you think Oscar has died and the loss has made me lose my mind a little. Tell them whatever it takes. Just get them to the mountains."

Jared reached out to gently touch Lily's cheek, his black sparkle standing out against her silver. "Ok. Just… keep yourself safe?"

Lily smiled, but couldn't respond honestly. Instead, she pulled back and glanced down at where Kiki and Jared's companion nuzzled heads together before it spread its wings and jumped upward into the trees, closely followed by the black feathered fairy.

"Lily." Yuri spoke in a softer voice than Lily had ever heard from her. "I'm sorry for banishing you. I was afraid I had signed your death warrant."

"If you hadn't, they would have killed me here." Lily smiled slightly. "I would have never learned the things I have."

"But you have suffered…" Yuri reached out to touch the bare side of Lily's head. "I'm sorry I couldn't have helped more."

"You're helping now. Look after Jared, and my parents."

Yuri nodded her ascent before spreading her soft butterfly-style wings and following Jared up into the trees.

"Are you sure about this?" Quinn asked as he approached Lily. Looking up into his topaz blue eyes, Lily swallowed past the lump in her throat.

"No." She admitted. "But it's the only idea I have. If you've got a better one, I'm all ears."

Quinn bit his lower lip for a moment before sighing and shaking his head. "Logically, it's a very good plan. If you can give them reasons to team up rather than fight, you may stand a chance of the majority of people realising they don't need to kill each other." Placing his hand on her head, he stroked her hair in a supportive manner. "I just know it's not going to be easy on you."

"Life has never been particularly easy." Lily shrugged.

"We could be the villains for you?" Axel suggested as he stepped closer. "We're not part of either race."

"The betrayal of me turning against my kind, my family, my friends will hit harder…" Lily shook her head. "Besides, I have a fitting background to turn me 'evil'. I've been insulted, abused, disrespected, mistreated, degraded, mutilated, hunted. It would be enough to make anyone angry enough to lash out." All eyes flicked down to the scars on her arms where the chunk of flesh still didn't quite match for the scar tissue, and up to the recovering burn on her head. Mutilated was an accurate term.

"Look," Lily cut off the men as they both went to speak. "It's not like I can turn back to anything anyway."

"She's right." Misha spoke up. "She's doing the most logical thing with the cards she has, and I'd like to offer up my cards to help as well."

"Thank you. If you guys are willing to help, I have ideas. However, we should probably get this done before the kingdom thinks Jared and Yuri are talking crazy. I want to keep the fire low but wide, so they have to fly up and away from it. That should keep them safe from the Densewood."

"Gotcha." Axel replied as the other two nodded. The three of them took off in different directions to make sure they could help control the fire as it took over the fairy kingdom.

Waiting until they were a decent distance away, Lily stood in the middle of the small clearing they had fought in and spread her arms out either side of her. Light pulled in and glowed around her figure while her eyes fell closed with focus. Uncontrollable fire like that she'd spread in Kita-Utara wasn't what she wanted, she needed the speed and heat of light to start a fire that was controllable by others. The light shot away from her at all angles until it hit a solid object. Upon impact, the light focused as if under a magnifying glass and set the bark, grass and foliage alight.

Taking a hold of the light that the fire produced, Lily was able to extend the effects around the trunks of the trees and have them infect the others close to them. Letting out a slow breath, Lily planted her feet solidly on the ground and drew the water within the woodland down through the roots of the plants and towards her.

"You're getting really strong..." Kiki whispered as she watched the fire spread while a wall of water rose from the ground around them until it reached Lily's waist. Lily curled a small smile at that, though her hands trembled a little from the amount of magic she was using at once.

"Let's just hope I'm strong enough to pull this off."

Glancing up at the yelling that floated through the air, Lily knew she was at least doing enough this time. The fire spread outwards quicker than it did upwards giving the fairies no choice but to abandon the cover of the trees. Even if the fire didn't eat its way into their homes, it was going to burn through the trunks and cause trees to fall like leaves in the autumn.

Fire crackled and the calls of the fairies grew quiet over the hours that passed. Lily froze some of the water which encircled her and Kiki to keep the heat on their bodies from getting too high. She couldn't afford to pass out this time.

After enough time, Lily followed the fire with the water she had accumulated, dousing the flames and revealing just how many branches and trees had fallen. The undergrowth had been burned away. The leaves had fallen leaving the woodland lifeless and charred.

Greyscale and silent. The Fae Greenwood was now a depressing sight. Some of the outer reaches of the woods had survived and only a small amount of the Densewood had been caught up with it.

It looked like death had visited without mercy.

The only patch of green which had survived was the small area where Lily had stood with her wall of water. One lone bluebell sat right on the edge of that patch, looking brighter than it ever would have done surrounded by colour.

Sitting down beside the flower, Lily ran her fingers over the petals gently.

"All the roots survived. The Greenwood will grow back." Lily whispered more to herself than Kiki who settled beside her reflecting the melancholy in Lily's heart. She had just destroyed a whole kingdom. Sure, this had been controlled unlike the destruction of the mansion in Kita-Utara, but it well and truly sealed her fate as a villain in the eyes of her kind as well as the eyes of the witches.

"Lil, are you ok?" Kiki nuzzled against her thigh. With the others nowhere to be seen, Lily let herself be vulnerable with the little cat, tears stinging her eyes.

"No." Lily whispered back, blinking back the tears before they could spill onto her cheeks. "It's logical as I'm already hated. But now I've given the world actual reasons to fear and hate me. We officially have nowhere to go back to, not even our parents."

"Well, I'm home so long as I'm with you." Kiki commented, jumping up onto Lily's lap reaching up to lick the tip of her nose comfortingly.

Lily pulled Kiki into a hug and buried her face into the soft fur. She had a point there. Lily would always have somewhere to belong so long as part of her soul was still alive in Kiki. The world wouldn't be fully dark until the mischievous light behind those bright eyes went out.

"That was insane!" An excited voice pulled her out of her mind; her ice blue eyes glancing up to see Axel and Misha making their way back towards her talking about how they had controlled the fire from going to the edges of the woodland. "You got skills with that wand."

"Why thank you," Misha bowed in jest, almost stumbling as she did so.

"They look like they had fun," Quinn spoke up from behind Lily, making her jump before turning to look at him. He had a mildly amused expression on his face but he didn't comment on her reaction. "We find ourselves with strange friends, no?"

"Agreed," Lily chortled. "I find most who befriend me are odd in some way." A small fond smile pulled on her lips as she thought back to Dia and Tanith who had been a little different than the norm. Even Finnigan had turned out to be 'odd', in a psychotic way.

"I, actually, had something to ask of you all." She continued once Axel and Misha were close enough. "I'm not going to be able to do this alone."

"We're with you." Misha smiled, though it faltered as Lily shook her head.

"No, I need behind the scenes help. I need stories to spread through the world to build up the fear of me, and then I need help pretending to be more impressive than I am." The looks of confusion were not lost on the fairy. Asking for help wasn't Lily's forte, she was beating around the bush and she knew it.

"What is it you need us to do?" Quinn asked patiently.

"I'm going to go and find the Morequacor. It might be able to help me deal with the Byrnes even if it's just by manipulating their minds to forget the eternal spell." Lily explained. "While I do that, I was hoping you all could travel in human form and spread the rumours of fire and death and chaos. Add fuel to the stories they already have but at the same time be there to help motivate people to accept the alliance of fairies and draconians when I come back."

"And of course, if you find a Byrne, keep an eye on them until Lily can turn up and make them 'disappear'." Kiki added.

"And what happens when you show up and have three races of people fighting back?" Axel pointed out.

"I'll have to be clever about how I show up in that case. Make it so they don't really know where the magic is coming from so they can't fight me personally."

"How?"

"I don't know." Lily admitted. "I'm making this all up as I go; I'm sure I'll figure something out. But stories and fear go a long way to making something worse than it is."

"We can always help the illusion if we are nearby…" Misha encouraged, her hand reaching out to clasp Lily's shoulder. "We'll also see if we can get anyone else on your side. I'll reach out to the other Byrnes who I know don't like the situation but are too scared to do anything. There's not many of them but it might help."

"Thank you," Lily smiled.

"Kiki," Axel addressed the feline. "If she needs help but is too stubborn to ask for it, you come find us ok?"

"Absolutely!" Kiki nodded, nudging the fist he held out with her head. Lily sighed at the exchange but it was certainly nice to think that maybe more people had her back than she thought.

Chapter 16: Mokai Omamake

After bidding farewell to one another, Lily watched Quinn, Axel and Misha vanish into the distance.

"So, how are we going to hunt down a legend not many have ever seen?" Kiki asked.

"With a lot of luck probably."

"We don't get much of that."

Lily chortled at the comment and nodded, Kiki had a point.

"When we escaped Mythanissiam and ended up on the beach, I thought I saw it." Lily admitted.

"What?! Why didn't you say something?"

"It's a legend, I thought I was hallucinating." Lily defended. "I thought I had resigned myself to death and so I was seeing Death's horse waiting for me."

"And now you actually have resigned yourself to die, you think you'll be able to find it?" Kiki asked bluntly.

"What? I'm not…"

"Lily." Kiki fluttered up to hover in front of her as she curled her lip. "You've just waged war on at least two races. You know we aren't going to survive this."

Kiki's green eyes met Lily's steadily until Lily couldn't hold her gaze any longer and looked away. "I know I've signed your life to this too, I'm sorry Kiki."

"I haven't once argued against it? I just want to make sure that *you* know what you are doing and are ok with it."

Lily smiled softly at the sentiment.

"Everything has felt hollow since Oscar died." Kiki continued. "I want the Byrne's to suffer or fail at the very least. I want mum and dad to be safe. I want Dia to be free of her father. I want Xalina and Tanith to be able to have their freedom as well as their relationship. I don't want everyone to live in fear of others like you have." Kiki butted her head gently against Lily's forehead. "I am by your side, one hundred percent of the way, until the day we can't go on any more. I will fight as best as I can and help every moment that I'm able."

"Ki…"

"You are so strong Lil, and I am so proud that I get to be your companion. I know Oscar felt the same." Kiki needed to stop. If she didn't, Lily was certainly going to burst into tears over the words that were considerably kinder than the ones living in her own head. "I just ask… that I get to scratch Finnigan's face plenty before we turn him into a mouse."

Lily couldn't stop the bark of laughter that left her as she watched the mischievous aura come back to Kiki who wiggled her eyebrows and flew back down to the floor with her head held high.

"Deal?"

"Deal."

Lily bumped her forehead against Kiki's with a small smile lingering on her lips.

"So, we start at the caves and work our way inland?" Kiki concluded as she slunk around Lily's shoulders and draped over one ready for the walk she obviously wasn't joining.

"And anyone we see, we scare," Lily agreed, finally taking a step off the patch of surviving greenery in her environment. Bluebells sprouted in wake of her feet, her magic instinctively trying to replenish the home she knew. She was tired though, and after a few minutes, the flowers stopped following her and faded into the distance.

"We can help with that."

Lily jumped at the rough, gravelly voice that growled through the charred world around her. Looking around, she spotted a skull looking back at her from a bundle of matted fur and debris. A wolf muzzle and face in skull form, furry ears flicking lazily above it showing she wasn't hallucinating. Orange eyes looked out from where there should have been hollow darkness and watched Lily with pinpoint focus.

"The Macellavir?" She whispered bemused.

"Not quite." The beast spoke, drawing itself to its feet and stretching. The pile of fur and debris, it surmised, was the other two Lily had seen, and she ended up being watched by another two skulls; the deer was just as off putting as the wolves. "Though, we are Death. Mokai Omamake to be precise."

Lily couldn't stop the instinctive step back she took as the beast closed the distance between them. She could feel the chill of lifelessness radiating off it. She was certain that if the ground beneath it hadn't been charred so badly, the beast would be leaving behind a dead footprint with each step.

"If you are Death, why would you help me stop a war?" Lily's voice cracked.

The wolfen beast sat in front of her, tall enough that its muzzle was level with her chest and the fluffy of its fur made it a bulk to get past.

"Tell me," It started. "What do you think 'death' is, fairy?"

Was that a trick question? Lily's eyebrow raised as she glanced at Kiki. Her mind went back to Oscar, and to those who had died in the fire she had set. Guilt and misery surrounded her heart as she answered.

"The end."

"Of one life, but it's also the start of another." The beast explained. "Souls don't die, they spend their time in a spirit world created and run by the gods of beginnings and endings."

"Gods?" Lily queried. Was this like the fables that ancient non-magic humans believed had control over their lives?

"Well, that's what they call themselves. They liked the word." The beast shrugged its shoulders as one of the others behind laughed lightly. "They are merely beings who help manage the balance of the world, though usually they are arrogant and annoying because they think they are important."

"Death," it continued, "is merely the movement of your soul away from the body it's currently in. We," it motioned towards the other two behind it who were closing in to join the conversation. "Are merely guides who watch over those close to death and help them move from this life to the spirit world."

Lily stood motionless for a moment with her mind attempting to catch up. Managing the balance of the world? If they'd never stopped the war, did that mean it just wasn't big enough to upset the balance? What even was 'balance'? Balance between what??

"So, you're here to guide me to my death?"

"No."

"To help with the balance of the world?"

"No."

"Then… what does this have to do with me?"

"Nothing. You freed us, therefore we owe you a debt."

Rolling her eyes, Lily shook her head. "Why couldn't you have just said that?!" The beast in front of her merely shrugged in response, gaining a small groan from the female. As if she needed more things to think about at this point in time! Though, she had to admit that having deathly companions around her would help with the image she was going to have to create.

"Weren't there five of you?" It was posed as a question,

but Lily would never forget how many had been there to tear Cyrus to pieces after they were freed.

"They went home."

"Ok." She said after realising she wasn't getting any elaboration on that response, "If you are Death, you must know where the Morequacor is?"

"Why would we?" The second lupine beast spoke, a touch of femininity to the growl.

"Because it's Death's horse?"

The cervine beast snorted in derision. "It is not. That thing was once a unicorn that's been mutilated by a parasitic abomination created by the gods."

Oh, this was all just too much. Lily hung her head forward and closed her eyes. "It's still the next part of my plan so I need to find it."

"Then maybe you are marked for death." The original beast spoke again. "Everyone who has dabbled with that creature has died. Cyrus would have done as well if he wasn't elongating his life and cheating death."

"Well, he's dead now because of the power he used." The second lupine beast snarled, causing a sickening shiver to run down Lily's spine at the memory. She never wanted to witness something like that again.

"If you do come with me, no more killing people… ok?" Her voice almost faltered at the orange eyes that settled on her. Who was she to tell death what to do? Still, she straightened her back to show her determination that her word was something she wanted to stick to.

"You think you can tell us what to do?" The cervine beast challenged.

"I don't imagine I could tell anyone what to do," Lily mumbled. "I'm asking you. Please. I want to find a way that doesn't cost any more lives."

"So naive," Cervine grumbled.

"Yes, but I think they'd like her." The first chortled, gaining a shrug from the second lupine beast.

"They would."

Who was 'they'? It didn't matter. Lily had too much to think about already, and right now she needed to keep moving. She wasn't sure how long she had left before this war was supposed to start, but having destroyed the fairies' home, it could theoretically start at any moment.

Lily needed to establish herself as the priority to stop.

"Ok?" She repeated, trying to keep herself looking confident in front of the horrific creatures. They surveyed her for a moment before nodding. Releasing a breath Lily did not realise she had been holding, she let herself relax a little. "Do you have names I can call you by?"

"Shi." The original and slightly larger of the two lupine beasts replied.

"Savu." The cervine beast informed.

"Marana." The second lupine beast said.

Nodding along with the names while trying to commit them to memory, Lily smiled softly. "Well, it's... nice to meet you all. I'm Lily, this is Kiki."

"Lily is a symbol of purity... you want to be evil, you are not to be pure." Marana informed her as they trotted closer and walked around her. "You should think about another name. Like, Rosa Black like the black roses of death?"

"I don't really want to change my name." Lily hesitated.

"It would be more for the stories that you want people to tell. If you grew black roses wherever you had been it would become an ominous tell that villainy had been around and that would help spread rumours and fear." Shi explained.

"That's not a bad idea." Kiki chimed in. "It would allow you to leave a mark without having to make huge scenes at times."

"Make them believe you could be right behind them and they would never even know." Savu added.

Lily nodded slowly at the idea. Any and all little tricks and illusions that helped her seem worse than she was were certainly worth trying. Especially if she left behind those black roses whenever she destroyed a location or took a Byrne out of the community.

"Ok. Black roses I can do." Lily finally agreed. "Ki, can you catch up with Axel and the others and let them know to add that symbol into the stories. Say there were black roses in the fires I've set, things like that."

Kiki nodded. "I'll meet you at the caves?"

"I wouldn't carry on without you." Lily leaned forward to kiss the feline's nose before she flew off to find Axel and the others. Lily turned back to the Mokai. "We should travel in plain sight but at a distance so the witches can spot us but not reach us."

"Yes. And you should ride me." Savu motioned to their back. "You'll look like you are in command of a steed of death while flanked by two deathly hounds."

"That would be an intimidating sight…" Lily mused. "Is it suitable for me to be on your back though?"

Savu snorted in laughter. "You are far too polite to be a villain." Lily flushed in embarrassment. Savu walked in front of her and motioned towards their back, signalling Lily to jump up. Awkwardly, and none too gracefully, she leaped up to flop over the creature's back before swinging a leg over and righting herself. Savu was considerably taller than Axel or Quinn had been and Lily could confirm that she felt more intimidating already being able to look down at others through the large set of antlers protruding from the top of Savu's skull.

Adjusting herself a little, Lily held out a hand towards the ground and focused until black roses began to pop up through the dead undergrowth. She continued until there was a small patch of them reaching back to the trails of bluebells. If anyone came to investigate, they would see the obvious change where she had walked.

Hopefully that would fuel the belief that she had changed and become darker as well.

Chapter 17: Morequacor

The journey to the caves was longer than the route she had taken previously. Mainly because this time she ventured out of the woodland and made herself visible to the witch villages. No, that wasn't quite right. She didn't just make herself visible on the horizon; the lupine Mokai made appearances in the villages before running back towards Lily.

Fear was what kept the war going. Therefore, fear was what Lily would take advantage of. Not that she knew if it was working, she had no one who could tell her what was going on as she moved to the southern beaches of their land.

It felt like an age since she had washed up on the shore after running from Finnigan. It was colder now than it had been then. Was it already approaching another winter? How long did that leave her before the war was supposed to start?

Pulling her eyes away from the distant shapes of Mythanissiam, Lily focused on the caves she had taken shelter in previously. If she was a legend in hiding, she'd probably choose the depths of caves whose entrances flooded every time the tide came in. They were cold, dangerous, and somewhere you'd naturally avoid.

"Lily!" Kiki screeched as she noticed them approaching. "Where have you been?!"

Lily caught the white-footed cat as she launched herself at the fairy. "Sorry," she started. "We took the long way in order to help spread rumours. Did you find Axel?"

"Of course. He and Misha have decided to travel together while Quinn is going in a separate direction." Kiki informed them. "They said they can spread rumours quicker. Quinn is going back to Kita-Utara to try and get Liserli on board too."

"With the fire I set there, it shouldn't be too hard to make the rumours say it was intentional and I intended to destroy the high ranked family." Lily mumbled bitterly at the thought of what she had done.

"Lily…"

"No," Lily stopped her, catching her own thoughts before they could spiral into voices once more. "I made this choice. This is the most logical idea that we have, we just have to become scary enough to keep the momentum going. I just hope the Morequacor can help us with the Byrnes."

"Still have no idea what to do with them?"

"I have suggestions…" Savu commented under their breath.

"We're not actively murdering people." Lily retorted sternly. "I hate the fact that some are already dead because of me."

"It would solve the problem."

"I said, no." Lily snapped.

Despite the eye roll she received from all the Mokai, they didn't continue to argue with her. Lily couldn't do it. She didn't want to hurt people, let alone kill them. If she did, she was lowering herself to a level she could never live with. It was bad enough that fire and screams haunted her dreams alongside shackles and cruel laughter.

Without waiting for anyone to speak again, Lily started into the cave, keeping Kiki curled in her arms for comfort. Not that the feline minded, after a few moments, her light purrs filled the ever-darkening cavern.

Once far enough inside, Lily created three orbs of light to float alongside them. One in front to see what was coming, and one either side so no one slipped down a hole or got cut by the jagged rocks sticking out from the uneven walls.

The cave path curved upward before delving downward at a steep elevation and for much longer than Lily would have expected.

"We must be completely underground by now." Kiki whispered, her voice still echoing off the damp walls. "It's a good thing the path went up first otherwise this would all be underwater."

"But when the tide is up, our exit will be completely gone and it's not like food grows here." Shi supplied.

"Then we'll have to make sure we aren't in here so long we run out" Lily commented before pausing mid step and turning to look at the Mokai. "Speaking of, I haven't seen you all eat anything?"

"We don't have to eat often." Shi explained.

"When we do, it's fresh meat." Marana continued with an ominous grumble. Lily had the feeling that if they truly got stuck in these caves, the Mokai would have little issue using her for a meal to keep them going until the next low enough tide to leave.

"Noted." Lily half squeaked, gaining an evil chuckle from Marana. The company Lily found herself in seemed to have evolved darker with each group. Dia and Tanith had been delightfully light. Axel and company had been jaded by the darker sides of life but still optimistic. These Mokai were only here because they had a debt to pay; once that was done, they would go back to their lives filled with the dead.

Lily just hoped she wasn't one of them.

Though, knowing the path she had chosen, it was becoming increasingly likely she would not survive it.

"Who are you?"

The new voice from the darkness pulled a yelp from Lily. Spinning around on the ball of her foot, she squinted into the darkness past the reach of the orbs. The voice was low, cold, sickly. It gave the feeling of something oozing down your spine, not enough to make you shudder but more than enough to make your entire body tense with anticipation and fear.

She couldn't see anything.

"I asked, who are you?" The voice was sterner, coming from behind them this time. Turning again, Lily yelled in pain as something flat and heavy connected with her forehead and knocked her onto her back, rocks sticking into her ribs and spine. Her head spun with the force of the strike and soon her chest was compressed by the inescapable pressure of a hoof pushing down on it.

Lily struggled as her ribs began to crack. Kiki and the Mokai were frozen in place and unable to help. The light magic she had been in control of vanished in a heartbeat.

The only light now was coming from that which held her down. A glow of indigo and dark violet shades lit up the cave slightly. The glow came from the mane, tail and wings of the beast. Its flesh appeared to be peeled back in places, revealing bone tendons and tattered muscle within the black coat. Half of its muzzle that drew closer to Lily's face lacked flesh, leaving areas of the jaw bare for bone and teeth to be seen.

A deafening crack sounded as her first rib gave way, thankfully too low to puncture a lung.

"Stop! I'm here for your help!" She yelled up at the equine face.

The descent of the hoof stopped but the pressure on the broken bone brought tears to Lily's eyes. Though, it was nothing compared to the pain which came next. Lowering its head, the Morequacor pressed the tip of its jagged and cracked horn to Lily's forehead.

Lily screamed as her entire body felt like it was taken

through flames and sub-zero temperatures and back again. She couldn't see. Her head was splitting.

Suddenly, light burst behind her eyelids. Images invaded her mind. Memories. It spiralled through her life like pictures in a flip book.

The years she spent trying desperately to keep up despite having no wings. The day she met Kiki and Oscar. The depth the bullying had reached.

Dia's laughing face. Tanith smirking. Kissing Finnigan. Being bound and having her magic drained. Blood dripping from her wrists as she awaited trial.

Kipar fixing her broken ankle. The book that had been filled with Litihana accounts of history. Finnigan slicing flesh clean off her arm. Being buried under snow. Tanith and Xalina in their own little world, lost in each other's eyes. The draconians who lost their lives in the raid.

The scroll of offensive spells. Dia's neck tattooed with failure. The illusions of the plains. The prison. The fire that had burned away the side of her hair for good. Oscar's grave.

The acts of near torture she had used on Lucretia in her grief. The hand that had sealed around her throat in Kita-Utara.

The fire. The smell of burning flesh she hadn't been able to register at the time. What was this? Mental torture? She didn't want to see all of this. Lily wasn't sure if she was still conscious. Would begging make it stop? Every image brought a fresh wave of pain.

The fire consumed her. It surrounded the faces of those she loved. Their screams were silent but the pain and fear on their faces was unmistakable. Why were they burning? Was it her fault? Had she done this too?

She hadn't meant to.

She was trying to save them. Seeing their suffering was worse than the pain burning through her brain.

Suddenly, the pain vanished and everything was dark.

"...ly." That sound was familiar. Though it was distant and dull, it was something that pulled on her consciousness.

"Lily!" Opening her eyes, Lily met Kiki's green eyes right above her in the dark. Pushing herself up to a seated position, Lily let out a long whine of pain as she went to clutch her ribs. When her fingers connected with skin, she snapped her attention down to herself. Her chest was bound tight with bandages from her satchel, her stomach on show and her shirt missing.

"Turns out, Shi wasn't lying... they do have human forms." Lily raised an eyebrow at the haunted tone of voice even if Kiki couldn't see it. "They kept the skulls..." Kiki whispered.

Behind Lily, laughter sounded out. "The look on your face was gloriously worth it though." Savu chortled. "Besides, you only need thumbs to tie bandages, a human face wouldn't be any help."

"Oh yes, because Lily waking up to a human with a deer skull for a head tying her up wouldn't just terrify her to death!" Kiki hissed.

"She didn't wake up."

"We weren't tying her up!"

"Ok! Please stop!" Lily called out, raising her hand to her head which throbbed excruciatingly. Taking a few breaths to steady herself, a light dripping noise further into the cavern felt like a hammer knocking against her eardrums. "What happened?"

"We thought it had killed you." Kiki admitted.

"I examined her past and her mind." A soft click of hoofs on stone neared, the purple glow from before lighting up the area in an indigo hue. The Morequacor came into view looking just as rotten and ominous as Lily recalled before her head had been invaded with pain. All her life she had thought she knew what nightmares were made of, but, between this and the Mokai who had chosen to journey with her, she realised that nightmares weren't what you expected.

"You," The Morequacor addressed Lily. "After everything you've been through and everything you've seen, you don't have any hate in you. Not even for Finnigan Byrne."

"What? Of course, she hates him!" Kiki protested.

"No. She does not." The way those purple eyes bored into her own, Lily realised what exactly had happened. This creature knew everything about her, what she showed outwardly and what she hid deep inside.

"But he lied to us, betrayed us. Mutilated us! He killed Oscar!" Kiki snarled.

"And yet, if she can save him, Lily will."

"I don't want anyone to die, especially not for a story they've been brainwashed into believing from childhood." Lily spoke up. "This war has destroyed so many and the children of the Byrne's are either too scared to go against them, or they are like everyone else and believe what they have been told all their lives."

"Lily!" Kiki sighed in exasperation. "We can't save everyone!"

"Why not?!" Lily snapped. "Why can't we work out ways to do the best for people rather than just writing them off as lost causes and signing death wishes?! I hate that I've already caused deaths! I didn't mean to hurt anyone in Kita-Utara, I hate that I reacted in a way that destroyed so much. I don't want to resort to that."

"And when he comes at you again with spells to slice your flesh off bone?" Kiki hissed, though when Lily remained silent the feline growled lightly. "I get 'not killing' as a go to solution, but if it's kill or be killed you better not choose someone like him over your own life!"

Lily remained silent.

"Lily! Promise me!" Kiki pleaded.

"I can't…" Lily whispered.

"Idiot!" Kiki spat before flying off further into the cave to get away from the conversation. Lily glanced around and found that the three Mokai were also looking at her with a judgment that clearly screamed they agreed with the feline.

"Perhaps you are foolish," The Morequacor continued, not seeming the least bit bothered by the mood in the cave. "But, it means you will not abuse the power if I help you."

Giving up on squinting through the darkness, Lily drew light from afar, pulling the rays through the labyrinth of caverns until they balled together above them all, bathing the cave in a warm yellow-tinged light.

"You'll help me?" She asked.

"I can offer you a power that will allow you to manipulate the minds of others." It explained.

"But... I don't want to manipulate others."

"Do you have another way to stop the Byrnes?" It deadpanned. "With this power you will be able to manipulate and change their memories, make them forget this spell and what this war is about. You will also be able to make people fear you more than they fear each other. You will be able to create illusions real enough to keep people occupied."

Lily's eyes widened at the explanation. That power sounded terrifying, but the Morequacor was right, it would give her the advantage she had been trying to get the whole time.

"If you take this power, it will kill you." The Morequacor continued. "It may be immediate, it may take years. The power isn't just magic, it is a parasite of sorts that will eat away at the magic in your body. The more magic you use, the quicker you will lose the ability to do so."

Silence fell over them as Lily went over the information she was given.

Her life wasn't as important as the lives of everyone else, even if she didn't want to die. She really didn't want to die. She also didn't want to lose her magic and be powerless. But how could she walk away now? This would give her what she needed to achieve her goals. She would be able to convince the Byrnes to go and start a new and kinder life. She would be able to make witches and fairies begin to see each other as allies rather than enemies. She would be able to make herself into a bigger threat than she really was and would ever be able to be at her age.

Closing her eyes, the images of her loved ones screaming in fire flickered across the darkness of her eyelids. She couldn't let them suffer. She couldn't abandon her plan now.

"I didn't expect to live through this anyway." Lily finally spoke, opening her eyes to meet the indigo hues of the Morequacor. "How do I accept it?"

"It might kill you straight away."

Glancing in the direction Kiki had left by, Lily let out a slow breath and nodded. "If it does, I will die trying my best."

"Sometimes people mistake kindness for naivety and bravery for idiocy." The Morequacor commented as it stepped toward Lily, each echo of hoof on stone sounding like steps taken towards the gallows. "Hold onto your kindness Lily Rosales, even if everyone hates you, hold onto what you know is good."

Once more the beast lowered its head toward her and the tip of the horn pressed into her forehead until it punctured the skin.

The pain from before paled in comparison to the feeling that exploded through her body. She could feel the invasion of another being in her blood, her body feeling too small to contain them both. Everything burned. She could feel her skin rupture on her left arm along the scars of her old wounds. Her insides felt like claws were ripping into them to make room for something else, while her tears fell from her cheeks and dripped bloody on the ground.

It was only as her sight began to fade that Kiki made it back to her, slamming into her chest and allowing Lily to cling to her as the pain grew to agony.

Lily doubted in those moments that she would survive, and if she did, she wasn't sure she'd ever be the same again.